THE LIBERATION OF JACOB NOVAK

NOVAK

AND OTHER STORIES

DON TASSONE

TOERNER PRESS

CONTENTS

ALSO BY DON TASSONE

Get Back

Drive

Small Bites

Sampler

New Twists

Snapshots

Francesca

Collected Stories

Musings

Journeys Within

Flash 50

Clara's Big Discovery

For Liz

"There's no path to liberation that doesn't pass through the shadow."

— Jay Michaelson

THE LIBERATION OF JACOB NOVAK

CHAPTER ONE

JACOB NOVAK HAD JUST FINISHED his shift at the coffee shop and was driving out of the parking lot when his RAV4 hit a pothole. He cursed as he hit the brakes, the jolt causing him to drop his cell phone.

Just two more weeks of this, he thought, then he would finally start college. For more than three years, he'd worked as a barista at The Daily Grind in Portage Park, near Chicago, to earn enough for tuition. He would be a freshman when many of his former high school classmates were seniors, but Jacob didn't mind. Keeping the real world at bay a little longer had been worth it.

He picked his phone up off the floor, made his way to the exit and turned onto North Cicero.

Jacob was nearly always on his phone when he drove, texting, posting messages, watching videos. Lately, he'd been watching the short videos that were constantly popping up on Facebook. Now he clicked on one featuring a UFC fight.

As he approached an intersection, Jacob glanced up and saw

the light turn yellow, so he gunned it. Then he looked back down at his phone.

Jacob didn't see the Prius, also trying to make the light, turn into his path. He rammed it, nearly head-on. His airbag inflated, snapping his head back against his headrest so hard he was knocked out. The smaller car spun around violently, slamming into his door.

Then everything was still. Someone called 911. Emergency vehicles were on the scene within minutes.

Both drivers were the only passengers in their cars. They were taken to Community First Medical Center. Jacob was rushed into surgery. The other driver, a woman, didn't make it.

CHAPTER TWO

THE FOLLOWING DAY, Jacob began to come to. He heard beeping. He tried to move, but something restrained him. His slightest movement sent a jolt of pain through his body. He moaned.

He heard footsteps coming toward him, then a familiar voice.

"Jacob, honey," his mother said, kissing his forehead. "Oh, thank God."

Jacob was Hannah Novak's only son. She had always been protective of him. His accident was a harsh reminder that her days as his protector had come to an end.

Looking down at him, broken, bandaged and casted, her heart hurt. Still, she felt relieved he was alive.

Jacob's eyelids felt like sandbags, but he managed to open them slightly. He saw his mother's face. She was crying.

"Mom," he whispered.

"It's okay," she said, gently stroking his hair. "You're going to be okay."

He opened his eyes a little more. His mother was dressed for work, as a nurse. At the edge of his field of vision, he saw a plastic IV bottle suspended from a metal hanger.

"Where am I?"

"You're in the hospital."

"What happened?"

"You were in an accident."

He tried to move again, but the pain along the left side of his body was searing. He winced and groaned.

"Just lay still."

Jacob was having a hard time staying awake. He closed his eyes and fell back asleep.

"How bad was I hurt?"

His mother had raised Jacob's bed, and he could now see around his room.

"You broke your neck, but it was a simple break, no spinal cord damage. Your left arm, left hip and left leg are broken, but they'll heal. You have lots of internal bruising. Fortunately, that will all heal too."

Jacob blinked. His mind was fuzzy. He tried to focus.

"How did it happen?"

"You ran a light at Cicero and Irving Park and hit a car turning left."

"Are they okay?"

His mother looked away.

"Mom?"

"There was only one person in the other car, a woman."

"Is she all right?"

"No," his mother said, her voice breaking. "She died on the way here."

Jacob gasped. He stared into his mother's face, then closed his eyes. He now remembered he'd been watching a video. The wreck was his fault. A woman was dead, and he was to blame.

"I'm sorry," his mother said, holding his hand. "I'm sorry."

Jacob felt like screaming but managed only a groan.

"Get some rest," his mother said, lowering his bed.

Jacob wanted to know more. For a moment, he fought to stay awake, but the strong meds coursing through his body overpowered him, and he fell back asleep.

When he awoke the next morning, Jacob saw his father sitting in the corner of the room.

"Dad."

"How are you feeling?" his father said, walking over to the bed.

"Hungry."

"They just brought your breakfast."

His father grabbed the food and placed it on the swivel tray over the bed.

"Do you think you can sit up?"

"I'll try."

His father pushed a button to raise the head of the bed. Jacob grimaced.

"Too much?"

"No, that's good."

His father removed the plastic covers from the food. Oatmeal, scrambled eggs and toast. Jacob slowly brought a spoonful of oatmeal to his mouth. Then he took a sip of coffee and made a face. It was lukewarm and tasted sour.

"Where's Mom?"

"Downstairs, working."

"What day is it?"

"Friday."

Jacob managed a bite of toast.

"Do you remember the accident?"

"No."

Silence.

"Actually, I do, sort of. I was watching a video on my phone. I wasn't paying attention."

"I know."

"You know?"

"Yeah. The police found your phone on the floor of your car. Apparently, a video was still playing."

Jacob took a sip of juice. His hand was trembling.

"Who was she?" he said.

"Her name was Alicia Rivas. She lived in Humboldt Park."

"Did she have a family?"

"Yes. A husband and two children."

Jacob felt a pounding in his head as he tried to grasp that reality. He'd not only killed someone but torn a family apart. Overwhelmed, he began to cry.

"It was an accident," his father said.

"No, Dad. I was watching a video on my phone! It was all my fault. I killed someone."

Jacob knew that texting while driving was illegal and figured watching a video was too.

"Am I going to jail?"

"I don't know, but I've been in touch with Henry Moyer."

Moyer had been Joe and Hannah Novak's attorney for years. Jacob had heard his parents mention Moyer but never knew what he did for them. He never imagined *he* would need a lawyer.

Nor did Joe Novak ever imagine his son would be in legal

jeopardy. There was hardly a day when he got home from work when Jacob wasn't up in his room. How could anyone who had lived such a quiet existence now be facing hard time?

Novak was deeply worried for his son, but he tried hard to appear calm.

"Have you talked with him about me?" Jacob said.

"Just briefly."

"What did he say?"

"He said there will be a trial and probably a lawsuit and that he would be willing to represent you."

Jacob imagined himself in a courtroom, being found guilty, going to prison. He felt fear rising within him. His mind was spinning. He felt dizzy. He closed his eyes and fell asleep.

His spoon slipped from his hand and fell to the floor with a clank. Jacob didn't move.

His father picked up the spoon, lowered Jacob's bed and turned off the overhead light. Then he sat back down in the corner, put his head in his hands and wept.

CHAPTER THREE

JACOB AWOKE in the middle of the night. His room was lit only by the soft glow from the screens of the medical devices at the head of his bed. The only sound was that of occasional footsteps in the hallway.

Jacob thought of the only person, aside from his parents, he had ever really loved. Her name was Sophia.

He thought of the first time he'd seen her. He was in kindergarten, eating lunch by himself, when a pretty girl he didn't know walked over and sat down across from him.

"My name is Sophia Diaz," she said with a smile. "What's your name?"

Jacob stared at her. She had dark hair, dark eyes and dark skin. Her eyes were big and bright. Jacob was mesmerized. He couldn't speak.

"You do have a name, don't you?"

"Jacob."

"Hi, Jacob. Are you in Mrs. Hudek's class?"

Jacob just stared at her with his mouth open a little.

"Are you in kindergarten?"

"Yeah."

"Well, then you must be in Mrs. Hudek's class. I'm in Miss Davis' class."

Jacob blinked.

"I live in Jefferson Park," she said. "Where do you live?"

Jacob shrugged.

She giggled.

"You don't know where you live?"

"Uh, Portage Park."

"Oh! I think that's close to me. We must be neighbors!"

Mrs. Hudek walked by.

"Five minutes, Jacob," she said.

He started packing up his lunch box.

"Do you want to have lunch together tomorrow?" Sophia said.

"Sure."

"Great. Adios!"

Jacob watched her, entranced, as she skipped away. He felt like he was floating.

The following day, Sophia came back, and they had lunch together again. And the day after that. And the day after that. Lunchtime became the favorite part of Jacob's day.

Jacob and Sophia became good friends, and they were close all through kindergarten and grade school.

Sometimes Jacob would go over to Sophia's house after school. He loved going there. Sophia had several brothers, who were loud and always in motion. Her parents spoke with a heavy accent. Sometimes they spoke a language that Jacob couldn't understand.

"They speak Spanish," Sophia told him. "They're from Guatemala."

Jacob had heard Sophia speaking this way around her family. To him, it made her even more fascinating.

One afternoon at Sophia's house, she said, "Would you like to paint?"

"I'm not sure."

"You're not sure? Don't you like to paint?"

"I haven't painted much."

"That's okay. I'll show you."

They went to her room. In the center was a card table with one folding chair. On the table were watercolor paints, pencils and a sketch pad.

"I'll be right back," she said.

She left and came back with another folding chair.

"Let's get some water," she said.

They went to the kitchen, filled two glasses with water and carefully carried them back to Sophia's room.

They sat down at the table. She opened the sketch pad and tore off two sheets of paper.

"Here you go," she said, sliding one over to him. "First we'll draw something, then we'll paint it."

Jacob wasn't sure what to draw.

"You go first," he said.

Sophia picked up a pencil and sketched a house. Around it, she drew trees and flowers. Jacob was amazed.

"Okay," she said. "Ready to paint. What are you going to draw?"

"I don't know," he said, staring at her drawing.

"Oh, come on. Think of something. Anything."

"I think I'd like to draw some trees."

"Cool. What kind of trees?"

"Apple trees, I guess."

He picked up a pencil but just sat there, looking at the blank paper.

"What's the matter?" she said.

"I've never drawn a tree."

"Here, let me show you."

She got up, reached by him and sketched the outline of a tree. As she did this, her hair brushed Jacob's face. It smelled like the roses his mother cut from her garden. Being that close to Sophia made Jacob tingle inside — and want to get even closer to her.

"That's all you need to do," she said, sitting down. "Draw a bunch of trees like that and add some apples."

Looking at the tree Sophia had drawn, Jacob copied it, slowly sketching half a dozen trees, with apples, across the page.

"Great," she said. "Now, let's paint."

They dipped their brushes in the glasses of water, then dabbed them on the watercolor tabs.

When they'd finished, she said, "Okay. Now let's sign our paintings."

"How?"

"I like to use black," she said, lightly dabbing the black tab in her tray and painting her name in block letters in the lower right corner.

Jacob carefully painted his name on his painting too.

"Wow!" she said. "Looks great!"

"Can I keep it?"

"Sure."

"Thanks," he said with a smile.

. . .

Jacob held his painting on his lap in the car on the way home. It was still drying.

"Did you do that?" his father said.

"Yeah. What do you think?"

"I think you're an artist."

When he got home, Jacob proudly showed his mother his artwork, then brought it upstairs and taped it on the wall next to his bed. He looked at it every day. Whenever he did, he thought of Sophia. That made him happy.

In sixth grade, Sophia and Jacob hit puberty. Sophia now had a boyfriend. All of a sudden, she paid little attention to Jacob.

Jacob felt slighted. Sometimes, he imagined being Sophia's boyfriend. He imagined being with her alone. He imagined kissing her, touching her.

Sophia still smiled at Jacob when she saw him in the hallways, but they now traveled in different circles.

They ended up going to different high schools. Jacob would look for Sophia when their schools played each other in football and basketball. She was easy to spot. She was a cheerleader.

He would come over at halftime and say hello. She always seemed happy to see him. She always gave him a hug. Jacob thought about asking her out, but he knew she had a boyfriend. Sophia seemed to have a lot of new boyfriends.

One morning, the summer after he'd graduated from high school, Jacob was preparing a buttered rum latte at The Daily Grind when he heard a familiar voice. He looked up. It was Sophia. She was standing in line, talking on her phone.

Jacob was thrilled to see her. But as she came closer, he grew concerned. She looked thin and tired. There were dark circles under her eyes. Jacob wondered if she was sick.

Sophia spotted him behind the counter, and her eyes grew wide.

"I have to go," she said, slipping her phone into her back pocket.

"Jacob!" she said with a small smile.

"Hi, Sophia. How are you?"

She stared at him intently, as if she were looking through him, and her smile faded.

"I'm getting married."

Jacob's heart sank. He knew he should extend his congratulations, but he couldn't speak.

"His name is Matt."

"Do I know him?"

"I don't think so."

Jacob looked down and kept working. When he looked up again, Sophia looked sad. Then she stepped out of line.

"It was good seeing you, Jacob," she said, as she headed for the door.

"Wait!" he said.

But she was gone.

He felt an urge to go after her. But what would he say? Forget Matt? Run away with me?

He spooned a layer of foamed milk over the coffee and sat the ceramic mug on the counter. A co-worker called out, "Buttered rum latte for Ashley."

As he started an espresso, Jacob wondered what was going on with Sophia. He hoped she was okay. He hoped he would see her again.

• • •

Now as he lay in his hospital bed in the darkness, Jacob wondered if Sophia was sleeping. He wondered if she was happy. He wondered if she ever thought of him.

CHAPTER FOUR

HENRY MOYER CAME to the hospital to meet with Jacob. He gently knocked on the frame of the open door and took a small step into Jacob's room.

"Hello," he said softly.

"Come in, Henry," said Jacob's father.

There was an earnest warmth about Moyer's face. He wore a suit and tie and carried only a thin briefcase.

"I'm Henry Moyer," he said, stepping over to Jacob's bed and extending his hand.

"Jacob Novak," Jacob said, taking it.

Moyer turned to Jacob's father.

"Joe, how are you?" he said, shaking his hand.

"I'm okay. Just concerned about Jacob."

"I understand. I'm here to help."

Moyer pulled a chair over to the bed, sat down and pulled a legal pad out of his briefcase.

"I'm very sorry about your accident," he said.

"Thanks," Jacob said.

"I want you to know everything we talk about today is privileged."

Jacob sensed he was in big trouble.

"Will I be sued?" he blurted out.

Jacob's father shifted in his chair.

"Probably," Moyer said. "What we know for sure is that you'll be tried in court."

"On what charge?" Jacob said.

"Reckless vehicular homicide."

"Will I go to jail?"

"If you're found guilty, yes, you'll have to serve time in prison."

"How long?"

"That depends."

"On what?"

"On what the judge decides."

"Years?"

"Unfortunately, yes. In Illinois, the sentence could be anywhere from three to 14 years."

Jacob gasped and looked over at his father. He thought his father might say something, but he remained silent.

"We'll argue for a lenient sentence," Moyer said.

"And I might be sued too?"

"Yes. Most likely for wrongful death."

"Does that mean more jail time?"

"No. It means money."

"How much?"

"Jacob," Moyer said, "these are all good questions, but we have lots of time to talk through everything and put together a plan. The only thing we need to prepare for right now is your arraignment."

"What's that?"

"That's when you're brought before the court to hear the charges against you and enter a plea."

"But how can I appear in court? I can't walk."

"I know. I'll arrange for a videoconference with the judge. It'll be brief. You won't need to leave your hospital bed, and I'll be right here with you."

"When?"

"Next week."

"Okay."

"The only thing we really need to discuss today is your plea," Moyer said.

"My plea?"

"Yes, how you'll plead at your arraignment."

"Guilty," Jacob said.

Moyer stopped writing. He'd never had a client who wanted to plead guilty. Jacob seemed sharp, but maybe the wreck had rattled his brain, he thought.

"Guilty?" Moyer said. "Of what?"

"Guilty as charged."

"Do you believe you were at fault?"

"Yes."

"Jacob, I've got to tell you a guilty plea is highly unusual these days."

"Why?"

"A not guilty plea buys time."

"Why would I need more time?"

"Well, it may not be you who needs more time. It might be me."

"Why would you need more time?"

"Jacob ..." said his father.

"It's okay," Moyer said. "We'll need time to prepare the best possible defense."

"But what I did was wrong," Jacob said. "It can't be defended. I'd rather have you focus on trying to get me less time in prison. Is that possible?"

"Well, if you plead guilty, the judge will certainly take that into account."

"If he pleads guilty, will there still be a trial?" Jacob's father said.

"No," Moyer said. "There will just be a sentencing hearing."

"And you think I might get a lighter sentence if I plead guilty?" Jacob said.

"Yes," Moyer said.

"Well, then," Jacob said, "that's what we're going to do."

Moyer was surprised. Most of his clients were deferential. He was used to negotiating with other attorneys, not his own clients, let alone one so young.

There's more to this young man than I thought. He's quiet, but he has a will of his own.

Jacob too was surprised. He had surprised himself. He was not used to asserting himself.

For most of his life, he'd gone with the flow. Aside from putting off college, he'd never really chosen a path for himself. Now here he was, on his own, telling a man much smarter and more experienced what path *they* should be taking.

Jacob wasn't sure what was happening or why. But he felt his self-confidence growing, and he liked the feeling.

"All right," Moyer said, putting his legal pad away. "I'll schedule a videoconference for your arraignment and let you know."

"Okay."

He got up and shook Jacob's hand.

"I'll see you next week," he said.

"Thank you."

He turned to Jacob's father.

"Please give Hannah my best."

"Thank you. I will."

When Moyer had gone, his father stepped over to Jacob's bed. Jacob noticed a puffiness around his father's eyes. His face looked thinner. He looked older.

"I know it's a lot to take in, but you will get through this," he said.

Joe Novak had faith his son would get through this ordeal, but the idea of Jacob being in prison made him want to die. He was such an innocent. How in the world would he survive in such a hellhole?

"Why don't you get some sleep?" he said, putting his hand on Jacob's shoulder.

"Okay."

His father lowered his bed and turned off the lights.

"I'll be right here," he said, sitting down in a recliner in the corner.

Jacob closed his eyes. He thought about his father and his mother too. He felt very grateful for his parents.

Then he thought about the children of the woman he had killed, how they would never see their mother again, how it was his fault and how he would have to bear the burden of that guilt for the rest of his life.

Jacob thought about all that lay ahead of him and wished he was the one who had been killed.

CHAPTER FIVE

"HOW MUCH LONGER WILL I need to be here?" Jacob asked his mother, who was sitting at the side of his bed.

"A couple more weeks."

"Will I be able to go home then?"

"No, you'll need to go to a rehab facility."

"For how long?"

"Probably a few weeks."

Aside from the beeping of monitors, Jacob's room was quiet. He felt fortunate to have a private room. It was comfortable enough, though he hated the antiseptic smell. He longed for the aroma of freshly brewed coffee.

Jacob looked over at his mother. She too looked older. He knew that, as hard as this was for him, it was even harder for her. This only added to his guilt.

"And then I'll be sentenced?" Jacob said.

"Mr. Moyer said your sentencing hearing won't take place until you're released from medical care. That means once your rehab is complete."

Hannah Novak was answering her son's questions. But she knew the unspoken question most on his mind. *Will I be okay?* It was her question too, but it was the one question she couldn't answer. All she could do was pray.

"Mom?"

"Yes?"

"Will you visit me in prison?"

"Oh, Jacob."

His mother began to cry. She got up and put her arms around him.

"Yes," she said, kissing his head and smoothing his hair, as she used to when was he was a boy.

CHAPTER SIX

AFTER HIS NIGHTLY MEDS, Jacob turned off the TV and the overhead light and lowered his bed. The soft lights from machines behind him shimmered like a phantom across the ceiling.

He felt uneasy. He was still thinking of his mother crying that afternoon. He hadn't seen her cry often. Whenever he did, he thought of when she told him about his sister, Emma.

Jacob was eight years old. He was watching TV when his mother turned it off and sat down next to him on the sofa.

"Jacob, I need to tell you something."

"What?"

His mother's hands were folded on her lap. He noticed they were shaking.

"I want you to know you had a sister."

Jacob wasn't sure he'd heard her right. He had always thought of himself as an only child.

"What?"

"You had a sister. Her name was Emma. She was born two years after you. She was stillborn."

"Stillborn?"

His mother sighed.

"Yes. Emma wasn't alive when she came out of my body."

Jacob was horrified by that thought. He wondered what happened to his sister. He had been to a cemetery. He wondered if his sister had a grave.

"Where is she?"

"Her body is buried in Niles, but her soul is in Limbo."

"Limbo?"

"Yes. She wasn't baptized."

"What's Limbo?"

"It's just outside of Heaven. It's a place of waiting."

"How long will she be there?"

"I don't know."

"Will she ever get to Heaven?"

"Yes, I think so," she said with a little gasp, "if we pray hard enough."

Tears ran down his mother's cheeks, and she started sobbing. It hurt Jacob to see her cry.

"I'll pray for Emma," he said.

"Oh, Jacob," she said, wrapping her arms around him, just as she had that afternoon.

CHAPTER SEVEN

——————

THE FOLLOWING THURSDAY, Jacob was arraigned.

Moyer had set up a laptop on the tray over Jacob's bed. Jacob sat upright in bed, and Moyer stood beside him.

The judge appeared on the screen and read the charges.

"How do you plead?" she said.

"Guilty," Jacob said.

The judge raised an eyebrow.

"All right," she said. "We'll schedule your sentencing hearing when your medical care is complete, Mr. Novak."

"Thank you," Jacob said.

"Thank you, Your Honor," Moyer added.

Alicia Rivas, the woman who died in the car accident, had lived in Humboldt Park, a neighborhood not far from Portage Park. As Moyer had predicted, her widowed husband, Jose, sued Jacob for wrongful death. He was seeking $500,000.

Moyer called Jacob to give him the news and ask if he could come to hospital that afternoon to discuss a game plan.

"Sure," Jacob said.

When Moyer arrived, Jacob was sitting in the recliner in the corner. He'd begun to shuffle around his room, using a walker.

"So what do you make of the half a million dollars?" Jacob said right away.

"He's fishing."

"Fishing?"

"He knows you don't have that kind of money. He also knows he can't show his wife's potential net worth would be anything close to that. He just wants to see what kind of a settlement he can get."

"Are we thinking about settling?"

"That would be my advice. But if we go for a settlement, we should make a low-ball offer and be ready to go up to an amount that you and I would agree to in advance."

"I've saved $75,000 for college. That's all I have."

"Well, we can offer $75,000, but we need to be ready to settle for twice that."

"And where would I get another $75,000?"

"Your parents."

Most of Moyer's clients were much older than Jacob. In the handful of court cases he'd handled for young adults, when they needed money, they quickly turned to their parents.

"My parents?" Jacob said. "They don't have that kind of money."

"Well, I happen to know they have a large retirement account."

"I'm not going to take a cent from their retirement account!"

This kid knows his mind.

"Okay," Moyer said, holding up his hand. "But we're going to need to get another $75,000 from somewhere."

"Do you really think Rivas will settle for $150,000?"

"I do."

"Why?"

Moyer felt like *he* was being cross-examined.

"Several reasons," he said. "First, $150,000 represents twice what we'll initially offer. Second, Mrs. Rivas had a high school education. She worked part-time in a dress shop. She made minimum wage. So it would be a real stretch for Rivas to make the case that his wife's earnings potential was more than $150,000. And third, $150,000 would be an enormous sum to the Rivas family. That's three times what Rivas himself makes in a year. I think he'd take it."

There was no way Jacob was going to ask his parents to pay for his mistake. Then he thought of another way he might get Rivas to settle for $75,000.

"All right," he said. "Let's go with your plan."

"Good."

I'm finally getting through to him, Moyer thought.

"I do have one request," Jacob said.

Crap, Moyer thought.

"What's that?"

"I'd like to meet with Mr. Rivas."

"What?" Moyer said, looking perplexed. "Why?"

"I want to apologize."

"Well, that's a noble thought, Jacob, but I wouldn't advise it."

"Why?"

"Because an apology is tantamount to admitting guilt."

"But I *am* admitting guilt."

"I understand. But I've never heard of a defendant in a

pending criminal case meeting with a plaintiff who's bringing a civil suit."

"Are you telling me I can't meet with Mr. Rivas?"

Moyer's ruddy complexion turned bright red. All his life, he had to work to control his anger. He was working hard to control it now.

"No, I'm not," he said sternly. "But I don't think it's a good idea."

"I understand," Jacob said.

There was an awkward silence.

"If you're serious about meeting with him," Moyer finally said, "I would insist on being there."

"All right. Would you set up a meeting for the three of us?"

"Yes," Moyer said, sounding unhappy.

There was a knock at the door. A nurse came in to give Jacob his afternoon meds. Her timing was good: it broke the tension.

Jacob knew he had pushed Moyer out of his comfort zone. He felt bad for doing that, but he also felt strongly about the need to meet with Rivas.

"Mr. Moyer, I have a question for you."

"Shoot," Moyer said, closing his briefcase.

"How did you become my parents' lawyer?"

Moyer looked at him and smiled. The redness in his face began to subside.

"My father and your mother's father were friends. They were both immigrants from Ireland. They met in Chicago before I was born. After Emma, your parents decided they needed a will. I was a young attorney building a practice, and my father recommended me to your grandfather, who told your mother. The first time I met your parents they brought you with them. You were a little boy. We got you some chocolate milk, as I recall. Anyway, I prepared your parents' will, and they've been my clients ever since."

"You've taken good care of my family for a long time," Jacob said. "Thanks for taking good care of me now."

"You're welcome, Jacob."

After Moyer left, Jacob thought about their exchange. He had no idea if meeting with Rivas would lead to a more favorable settlement. But there was a more important reason he wanted to meet Jose Rivas.

CHAPTER EIGHT

JACOB HAD MOVED to a private room in a nearby rehab center. He spent much of his time there sitting in a recliner, usually watching TV.

He was sitting there when Rivas arrived for their appointment. Moyer sat next to him.

Rivas knocked lightly.

"Come in," Jacob said.

Jacob gripped his walker and slowly got to his feet. Moyer stood up too. Rivas stepped in tentatively. His eyes darted around the room. He looked wary. Jacob noticed his light blue dress shirt had square creases all over it, as if it had just been purchased and not yet laundered.

"Mr. Rivas, I'm Jacob Novak."

Rivas stood still for a moment, staring at Jacob, before coming over and shaking his hand.

"Mr. Rivas, I'm Henry Moyer, Jacob's attorney."

Rivas shook his hand too.

"Please have a seat," Moyer said.

Rivas pulled over a high-back chair, and the three men sat facing each other. None of them looked comfortable.

"Thank you for coming," Jacob said.

Rivas nodded.

"I asked you to come here for two reasons," Jacob said. "First, I want to tell you how sorry I am for the loss of your wife."

"Thank you," Rivas said with a heavy accent. "Alicia was the great love of my life."

"I'm sure she was," Jacob said.

There was an awkward silence.

"And the second reason?" Moyer said.

"Yes," Jacob said. "I also want to ask your forgiveness."

Rivas looked at Moyer.

"What I have to say today isn't a legal matter," Jacob said. "I'm speaking from my heart."

Rivas kept his eyes on Moyer, as if he were suspicious that the whole thing was a setup.

Sensing his unease, Moyer got up.

"Gentlemen, I think this is a matter strictly between the two of you. So I will excuse myself."

He walked out.

Jacob was surprised. After all, Moyer had insisted on being there. Maybe he felt he could trust Jacob. Or maybe he was fed up.

Regardless, Jacob was now on his own. This was his meeting. He had called it for a reason, and now he needed to see it through.

He looked Rivas in the eye.

"Mr. Rivas, I am the reason your wife is no longer here. I hope God will forgive me, but if he does, that still won't be enough. I am asking for your forgiveness as well."

Rivas looked away. His face was flushed. He got up and walked over to the window. He stood there, his arms crossed, looking out.

"Do you realize what you've done, what you've done to my family, to my children, to me? You've torn us apart. Now my children will have to grow up without their mother. Alicia was everything to me. Now, because of you, I'll never see her again. And you're asking me to forgive you? You killed my wife because you weren't paying attention while you were driving. You were watching a f**king video. My wife is dead because you were watching a f**king video instead of paying attention. And now you ask me to forgive you? You ask too much."

"I understand how you feel, Mr. Rivas."

"Do you?" Rivas said, turning toward Jacob. "How can you possibly know how I feel? How can you ..."

Rivas dropped his head and closed his eyes. He stood there, his arms still crossed, saying nothing.

Jacob wasn't sure what to say. He didn't want to say anything that would make Rivas even more upset.

"Mr. Rivas, may I ask you something?"

Rivas looked up.

"What?"

"Your children, what are their names?"

The question seemed to catch Rivas off-guard.

"Anna and Santiago," he said quietly.

"I understand if you can't forgive me," Jacob said. "But will you please tell your children I'm sorry?"

Rivas' expression softened.

"Yes," he said, nodding. "I will."

Then he said, "I should go."

Jacob reached for his walker.

"Don't get up," Rivas said.

"Thank you for coming here today."

Afterwards, Jacob was despondent. He had been sincere in his request of Rivas, but he had underestimated the depth of his anger. Rivas was right, of course. Jacob did kill his wife, and maybe there was simply no forgiving anything so terrible.

I am naive, Jacob thought. He'd been living a virtual existence. He wondered if he would ever understand the ways of the real world. *I should have listened to Moyer.*

But the following week, both Jacob and Moyer were stunned when Moyer received a letter from Rivas' attorney saying his client agreed to settle his lawsuit for $75,000.

"You were right," Moyer said.

"But I didn't ask Rivas' forgiveness so he would settle."

"I know. But you were right."

Jacob knew this would now wipe out his savings. He would have to start all over when he got out of prison.

But he knew it would also mean his parents' retirement fund would remain intact. Even more important, he felt it was the beginning of atoning for his great sin.

Having settled Rivas' lawsuit before his sentencing hearing was definitely a point in Jacob's favor.

"The judge will be impressed," Moyer said.

"Do you think I'll get a lighter sentence?"

"Yes."

Jacob looked at Moyer. He felt lucky to have such a good lawyer, a true expert who also respected his wishes.

"At the sentencing hearing, will you be speaking for me?"

"Yes, I'll make a statement on your behalf."

"What will you say?"

Moyer thought for a moment.

"I'll point out you have no prior offenses and that you've conducted yourself admirably, taking full responsibility for your actions and offering Mr. Rivas a generous settlement, which he has accepted. I'll remind the judge you're only 21 years old. You have your whole life ahead of you. You're willing to pay your debt to society. But the sooner you're released from prison, the sooner you can become a fully contributing member of society."

"And you think I'll get a lighter sentence?"

"I do, along with the possibility of parole."

Moyer's confident tone bolstered Jacob's confidence.

"Okay," he said. "Let's go for it."

CHAPTER NINE

JACOB HAD JUST FINISHED breakfast when he heard a light knock on his door.

"Come in."

The door opened slowly.

"Hello."

It was *her* voice. Then he saw her face. It was Sophia.

She looked even lovelier than he remembered. She was wearing a white sweater and blue jeans and holding a bouquet of flowers.

His heart raced.

"Sophia," he said, grabbing his walker and standing.

"Oh, Jacob. I just heard about your accident. I hope you're okay."

"I'll be fine."

He looks so thin, she thought. Then she smiled and stepped over to him, and they embraced.

She was softness, and her hair smelled like roses. It

reminded him of when they were children. Her scent made him feel warm inside.

Holding hands, they stepped back from one another. She still had circles under her eyes, although much less dark than when he'd last seen her in the coffee shop. But her brown eyes were bright again. This made Jacob happy.

"It's so good to see you," he said.

"It's good to see you too."

"Please sit down," he said, motioning to a chair.

"Thank you."

She looked around and laid the bouquet of flowers on the tray next to his bed.

"I'll find a vase for those later," he said.

She stepped back over, pulled a straight back chair close to his recliner and sat down.

There was so much to say, but they looked at each other and said nothing. Her eyes welled with tears.

"It's okay," he said, blinking back his own tears. "It's okay."

She pulled out a tissue and wiped her eyes.

"I'm sorry," she said. "It's just that so much has happened."

"Yes."

Regaining her composure, she said, "Please tell me what happened, if you're comfortable."

"Sure."

He told her about the accident and how he had been watching a video on his phone. He told her he felt devastated he had killed someone and that he'd asked Jose Rivas to forgive him. He said he would be sentenced when he was released from rehab and would have to serve time in prison.

"I'm so sorry," she said, reaching out for his hands.

They held hands and looked into one another's eyes. How he

had longed to see her again. How grateful she was that he was alive and on the mend.

She let go of his hands and sat back in her chair.

"When I last saw you, in the coffee shop, I was pregnant," she said. "I felt I had to get married. I wish I hadn't. My husband was, well, abusive. I divorced him."

"I'm sorry," he said. "And your baby?"

Her face lit up.

"It was a boy. His name is Mateo. He's three years old now. He's the light of my life."

"Congratulations. I'm happy for you. Where do you live?"

"We live in a small apartment in Old Irving Park."

Jacob knew that neighborhood well. He had just turned off of Old Irving Park Road when he had his accident.

Sophia went on to say she was working at Marshalls.

"I don't love the job, but it pays the bills and has health insurance."

"I'm proud of you," Jacob said. "And I'm glad you and Mateo are okay."

"You're sweet. You were always sweet."

Jacob smiled.

"I have a silly question," he said.

"What's that?"

"In kindergarten, the day we met, why did you come over and sit with me at lunch?"

She smiled and blushed.

"I've wondered about that myself. I don't know exactly. All I can say is that I felt drawn to you."

"I know the feeling. That was one of the happiest days of my life."

"I've missed you," she said, reaching out for his hand again.

"I've missed you too."

They sat there, holding hands, until she said, "Well, I'd better get going."

They got up and embraced, and he kissed her on the cheek.

"Thank you for coming," he said.

"Take good care. I'll see you again soon."

He watched her walk to the door, then turn and smile before she slipped out. In that moment, he felt no pain, only joy, and he wondered if they could ever be more than friends.

CHAPTER TEN

JACOB DREAMED about being on a small motorboat on the water. He looked around. He was in a harbor. Through a light fog, he spotted two people standing on a dock, waving and calling his name. Their voices were familiar.

He steered his boat over to them. As he got closer, he realized they were his parents. They looked happy to see him.

His mother cradled a sleeping infant in her arms. Somehow, he knew it was Emma.

Without words or instruction, Jacob knew what to do. He maneuvered his boat alongside the dock so that it very slowly glided up to his parents. Carefully, his mother handed Jacob her baby.

"Take her home," she said.

His father simply nodded.

Holding Emma, Jacob sat back down in the driver's seat and glanced goodbye to his parents. He turned the wheel, pushed forward the throttle lever slightly and headed out into the harbor. He went slowly so the sound of the motor wouldn't wake his sister.

Through the fog, Jacob could see a bright, pulsing light. As he got closer, he realized it was coming from a lighthouse at the edge of the harbor. He could see open water just beyond. Was this his destination? Jacob wasn't sure, but he kept going.

But when he had almost reached the lighthouse, Jacob woke up. He looked around his room, then closed his eyes, wanting to finish the dream.

He fell back asleep but, as dreams do, this one drifted away.

CHAPTER ELEVEN

AT HIS SENTENCING HEARING, Jacob's parents sat in the bench just behind him, who sat next to Moyer at the defendant's table.

The only other people in the courtroom were the prosecuting attorney and Jose Rivas, who sat behind the plaintiff's table.

When the judge came in, everyone rose. Sitting down, the judge said, "Mr. Novak, counselors ..."

Everyone but Moyer sat down. He then made a statement on Jacob's behalf, making his case for a reduced sentence and the possibility of parole. Then he sat down.

All eyes were on the judge.

"I agree," she said, cutting to the chase. "Mr. Novak, I order you to serve three years in the Chicago Metropolitan Correction Center with the possibility of parole."

Moyer put his hand on Jacob's shoulder.

"Thank you," Jacob whispered.

A security officer stepped over. Jacob was still using a cane, so there were no handcuffs. The officer motioned toward a door along the back wall.

"This way," he said.

"May I have a moment, please?" Jacob said.

The officer nodded.

Jacob turned around and faced his parents. They looked anguished. His mother was crying. Jacob felt ashamed.

"I'm sorry," he said.

"We love you," his mother said.

"Take care of yourself," said his father.

Then Rivas caught Jacob's eye. Jacob was surprised to see him. Rivas looked solemn, his hands folded in front of him, as if he were in church. At that point, the courtroom was as quiet as a church.

"I'm so sorry," Jacob said.

Now all eyes were on Jacob and Rivas.

Rivas just stood there, staring at Jacob. *Is he here just to see me get what I deserve for killing his wife?* Jacob thought. *Does he want to watch me be taken away? Is he here for revenge?*

Finally, Rivas said, "I forgive you."

Jacob was stunned. In the drama of the moment, he had forgotten he had asked for Rivas' forgiveness. Now here he was to grant it at the very moment when Jacob was about to begin his atonement, his lowest point, when he most needed to hear those words from the soulmate of the woman whose life he had taken. They felt like a blessing.

"Thank you," Jacob said.

Rivas simply nodded.

"This way," said the officer.

Jacob turned and followed him through the door.

CHAPTER TWELVE

STEPPING inside the Chicago Metropolitan Correction Center, the MCC, Jacob was immediately struck by the smell. It was as musty as an old cellar. He got the sense the whole place could use a good cleaning.

He shared a cell with a 49-year-old former business executive named Jack Dawson. He'd worked in finance for a big food company. He was serving time for embezzlement.

Dawson was short and slight, with thin, mostly gray hair. He wore wire-rimmed glasses. He looked like a man who was comfortable wearing a suit.

Jacob had imagined the guys in prison were all uneducated jocks. He hadn't expected to see anyone as frail and refined as Dawson. He was relieved to have a cellmate much smaller and older than he was.

Dawson immediately called him Jake. No one had ever called him that.

As soon as they met, Dawson said, "You can have the top bunk." Jacob assumed it was his way of saying he was in charge.

Dawson talked a lot. He didn't bother to ask Jacob anything before launching into his own biography. First in his family to go to college. MBA from Chicago Booth. Hired right out of graduate school by Mullins Foods, where he worked his way up to director of finance. Two kids. Divorced. Used to drive a metallic red BMW 4 Series convertible.

Dawson's career came crashing down when the cops showed up at Mullins one day and arrested him. He was charged with embezzling half a million dollars. The sentence for such a crime in Illinois is four to 15 years in prison and up to $25,000 in fines. Dawson hired an expensive attorney who struck a bargain for seven years and a fine of $10,000. He seemed particularly proud of his "light" fine.

When it came to why he'd stolen the money, Dawson blamed everyone but himself. His parents had never given him an allowance. They'd never taught him "the value of a dollar." His wife had champagne tastes. He was consistently underpaid, and he was only compensating for all the raises he never got over 25 years. He even criticized his bosses for not having caught him sooner.

Dawson shared all this having just met Jacob. It was as if he wanted him to know his story right up front. The way he spoke, so glibly, made Jacob think he had told this story many times before.

And he said it all without a trace of compunction. Jacob didn't consider himself virtuous. But when he did something wrong, he admitted it and felt bad. Dawson was found guilty of embezzlement, and the only thing he seemed to feel bad about was not getting a shorter sentence.

Jacob was glad his cellmate wasn't a convicted murderer. But there was something about Dawson that made him uneasy.

After only an hour, he wasn't sure how much more of his crap he could take.

The MCC was a 27-story skyscraper in downtown Chicago. It housed more than 600 inmates. Most shared a small cell with no bars. Instead, each cell had a floor-to-ceiling slit window, seven feet long and five inches wide, beveled out to allow natural light to pass inside.

The most unusual feature of the prison was the exercise yard. It was on the roof. The rooftop was hemmed in by 30-foot concrete walls with small, fenced openings. On the eastern side of the roof, through those openings, prisoners could see the Chicago Harbor and, just beyond it, Lake Michigan.

Jacob's first prison meal was dinner. Entering the "chow hall," he found the size and noise daunting. It was a sea of men in orange, eating, talking and yelling.

Jacob tagged along with Dawson. He followed him through the food line and sat next to him at a table, where six men were already eating.

"This is my new cellmate, Jacob Novak," Dawson said. "Three years for vehicular homicide, with the possibility of parole."

"Bullshit," said a burly, middle-aged man sitting across from Jacob. "Ain't no such thing as parole around here."

"Shut the f**k up," said a man sitting next to Dawson. "You trying to kill this guy's spirit on day one?"

"F**k you," said the middle-aged man.

"I'm Brody," he said, extending his hand across the table.

His arm was a sleeve of black and blue tattoos, mainly snakes coiled around each other.

"Hi," Jacob said, taking his hand. "I'm Jacob."

"Call him Jake," Dawson said.

The MCC served only two meals a day. Breakfast and lunch were clumped together. Everyone at the table ate hungrily. Jacob thought the others might introduce themselves, but they kept eating and, between bites, arguing about baseball.

Jacob quickly realized "f**k" and all its derivatives were part of the MCC vernacular. He also learned the guys at his table were either Cubs or White Sox fans.

"What about you?" Brody said. "Cubs or Sox?"

Jacob wasn't a big baseball fan, and he didn't have a favorite team. But he knew the White Sox were usually an underdog. He felt like an underdog, especially at that moment.

"Sox, I guess," he said.

"F**k the Sox."

"F**k you."

For the rest of the meal, no one spoke to Jacob. He wasn't sure what to make of that. Maybe he checked out. Maybe they weren't interested. Or maybe they were just hungry.

When they got back to their cell, Dawson said, "Good job, kid."

"What do you mean?"

"Not saying much. Nobody likes a loudmouth."

CHAPTER THIRTEEN

A FEW DAYS LATER, Jacob got a card. When he saw "Sophia Diaz" in the upper left corner, his heart skipped a beat.

He climbed up to his bed, tucked his pillow behind him and leaned back against the wall. He carefully opened the envelope and pulled out the card.

It was white with a small, embossed heart on the front. He opened it and read the handwritten note inside.

Dear Jacob,

I hope you are well. Please know you are in my thoughts and prayers.

I will visit soon. In the meantime, I hope you'll write.

Take good care.

Your friend,
Sophia

Jacob closed his eyes, tilted his head back and recited Sophia's words in his head. *Please know you are in my thoughts and prayers.*

For a moment, he was no longer in prison. He was with Sophia.

The following day, Jacob bought stationery, envelopes and stamps in the commissary.

That afternoon, he climbed up to his bed and wrote this letter.

Dear Sophia,

I hope you and Mateo are well.

Thanks so much for your card. You are in my thoughts too. I do hope you'll visit.

In the meantime, please know I am fine.

Take good care.

Your friend,
Jacob

It was the first physical letter he'd ever written. There was so much more he wanted to say to Sophia, but it was a good start.

He addressed an envelope, folded his letter carefully, slipped it inside and affixed a stamp.

On his way to dinner, Jacob dropped it in the mail. As he did, he asked God to take good care of his friend.

CHAPTER FOURTEEN

JACOB SOON BEGAN GOING up to the exercise yard. His cell was on the tenth floor, and inmates had to use the steps to get up there. Walking up 18 flights of stairs was itself quite a workout.

Jacob was no longer using his cane to get around the prison, but he needed it to go up and down those steps. Once he made it to the roof, he had to hand his cane, a potential weapon, to a guard.

When he started going up to the rooftop, Jacob walked slowly around the perimeter. It was a new form of PT, without a physical therapist, of course. Day by day, he gained strength and speed. After a couple of weeks, he no longer walked with a limp. It had been nearly hour months since his accident. Sometimes his left leg was sore, but Jacob felt healed.

The main form of exercise on the roof was basketball. One sunny day, after walking five laps, Jacob took a break. He leaned against the wall, watching five guys shoot hoops. He didn't know them, but the distinctive tattoos on their necks and arms looked familiar. He'd seen them around.

"Hey, punk!" one of them yelled.

He was Black, shorter than Jacob but twice as wide and all muscle. He looked like a linebacker.

"You in?"

Jacob had played basketball in gym class in high school, but he'd never played on a team, and his skills were very basic. These guys looked like pros. He shook his head.

"Come on!" the linebacker said. "We need one more."

What the hell.

"Okay," Jacob said.

"Cool," said the linebacker.

He threw the ball to Jacob, hard. It bounced off his chest, but he managed to hang onto it. He wasn't sure what to do with it, though.

"Put it up!" somebody yelled.

Jacob dribbled twice, then shot. The ball fell way short of the basket.

"Damn!" the linebacker said. "You guys get the punk."

They quickly divided into two teams of three and started a game. The play was rough. This was street ball. Jacob was like a boy among men.

He was standing near the basket. He was open, and someone threw him the ball. Jacob pivoted and was about to shoot when a huge guy, even bigger than the linebacker, shoved him hard from behind, knocking him to the ground.

"Hey!" the linebacker shouted. "What the f**k!"

The bully who clobbered Jacob was white. He looked like a WWE wrestler. A fierce-looking dragon tattoo ran up the back of his neck and over his shaved head.

The linebacker ran over and knelt beside Jacob, who sat stunned, his mind reeling.

"Kid, you can't let this go," the linebacker said in a low voice. "You gotta stand up for yourself or Godzilla will make you his bitch."

Jacob wasn't sure what to do. The idea of standing up to this monster terrified him, but he sure didn't want to be anyone's bitch.

He got up and glared at the bully.

"Is that the best you can do?" Jacob said.

Godzilla growled and came at him. He pushed Jacob down hard, knocking him to the ground again.

"Get up," the linebacker said.

Somehow, Jacob managed to stand.

"Come on," he said. "You can do better than that!"

Enraged, Godzilla clenched his fist and took a roundhouse swing at Jacob's head. He got his arms up just in time to deflect the punch, but the force of it knocked him to the ground again. This time, his head hit the pavement, knocking him out.

Again, the linebacker knelt beside Jacob. When he didn't move, he shouted, "Guard! Man down!"

A guard slowly made his way over.

"Back away, all of you!"

Everyone moved back. The guard crouched beside Jacob and put two fingers on the side of his neck.

"Can you hear me?" he said.

Jacob still didn't move, and there was no response.

"What happened?" the guard said, looking around.

"He fell," somebody said.

"Bastards," the guard mumbled.

He stood up and called for help on his walkie-talkie.

"Time's up!" he yelled. "Line up!"

Two other guards, batons in hand, moved the inmates toward the door. The linebacker, though, took a step back toward Jacob.

"What do you think you're doing?" the guard said.

"Is he okay?" said the linebacker.

"He's breathing. Help is on the way. Now get in line."

A few minutes later, a helicopter landed on the roof of the MCC. Jacob began to come to. Two EMTs checked him out, put him on a stretcher and loaded him into the chopper.

The chopper took off for Northwestern Memorial Hospital, less than two miles away. There, Jacob underwent X-rays and was treated for a concussion and a broken right forearm. His head wound required only cleaning and dressing. His arm needed a cast but no surgery. He was admitted for observation overnight.

That night, looking around his room, everything seemed familiar to Jacob. He had spent most of the past four months in the hospital or rehab. And now he spent most of his time in a prison cell.

His life had come to a standstill. Even if he could fast forward it, beyond prison, what would he do? Make lattes? Was that his future?

Jacob had always been aimless. But he always assumed that, at some point, his purpose would become clear to him.

Now, though, he wasn't sure he had a purpose or if life was even worth living.

CHAPTER FIFTEEN

AFTER BREAKFAST THE FOLLOWING MORNING, Jacob was released. He rode back to the MCC in a prison van.

His casted arm was heavy, but Jacob could walk on his own. A guard escorted him to his cell. When he got there, Dawson was sitting against the wall on the top bunk.

"I heard you got roughed up," he said. "I'll take the top bunk for a while."

"Thanks."

In the lunch line, Jacob sensed everyone was looking at him. He assumed they were checking out his cast.

"What happened on the roof?" Brody said as Jacob sat down at the table.

"I was playing basketball. Godzilla clobbered me."

"I heard you stood up to him," Brody said.

"Yeah."

"You got balls, man," said another of the regulars. "Way to go."

It was the first time any of his table mates had asked Jacob anything. It felt good.

After lunch, in the rec room, when Jacob was about to head back to his cell, the linebacker approached him.

"Hey, man. You okay?"

"Yeah."

"Broken arm?"

"Yeah."

"You did good, kid. You stood up for yourself."

The linebacker smiled. One of his front teeth had a gold cap.

"I'm Bruno."

"I'm Jacob."

With his cast down to his fingers, he didn't even try to shake hands.

"Sorry I got you into that mess," Bruno said.

"You didn't, and you gave me some good advice. Thanks."

"No problem. You ain't played much basketball, have you?"

"No."

"Well, you keep playin like you did the other day, and you're gonna get killed. If you want, I can teach you a few things."

"Great."

"When do you get that cast off?"

"In about a month."

"Good. We can start then."

After that, one by one, Jacob's table mates introduced

themselves. Not while they were eating. In the lunch line or rec room.

Their names were Barlow, Finn, Dax, Omar and Rigs. Jacob wasn't sure if these were their first or last names or even nicknames. But everybody went by just one name. In the MCC, his was Jake, and they all now called him by name.

CHAPTER SIXTEEN

ONE MORNING in the exercise yard, as Bruno and others were playing basketball, Jacob walked over to one of the small fenced openings along the eastern wall of the prison and looked out.

Beyond the buildings far below, he saw water, lots of water. He realized he was looking at a harbor and, just beyond, Lake Michigan. Boats dotted the harbor, and boats and ships traversed the lake.

Jacob imagined what it would be like to be out on the open water. How good the sun, wind and spray must feel.

That day, he started thinking about buying a boat when he got out of prison. He knew it might be a long shot. But for the first time in his life, Jacob had something to look forward to, and that made his heart feel light.

CHAPTER SEVENTEEN

JACOB WAS READING IN BED. Dawson was in his bed up top, droning on once again about how Mullins had screwed him. Jacob couldn't take it anymore.

"Bullshit," he said.

"What?"

"You heard me."

"What do you mean?"

"You know, Dawson, you blame everybody but yourself for your situation."

"You little shit."

"Call me what you want. But I know why I'm in here. I killed somebody, and I'm paying for it."

"You screwed up."

"I made a bad choice."

"And you think I made a bad choice?"

"Yeah, I do."

"F**k you. If it wasn't for those bastards at Mullins, I wouldn't be in here, talking to a loser like you."

After that, Dawson didn't say much to Jacob. He stopped sitting next to him in the cafeteria too.

CHAPTER EIGHTEEN

AS JACOB WAS COMING BACK to his cell after breakfast, the cell block guard said, "You got a visitor coming tomorrow, Novak."

"Who is it?"

"Somebody Diaz."

Jacob's heart raced.

That afternoon, he got a haircut and picked up a clean jumpsuit. The following morning, he shaved and showered.

That afternoon, Jacob sat on a chair in the common area, waiting for Sophia to arrive. His armpits felt wet. He took deep breaths to try to calm himself. He watched more than a dozen people file through the door.

Then he saw Sophia. She was wearing a light blue dress and a white, cardigan sweater. Jacob stood up. Sophia looked around but apparently didn't spot him in the small sea of orange jumpsuits.

"Sophia!" he called, waving to her. He wanted to go to her but had set aside a chair for her and didn't want to risk someone taking it. Fortunately, she finally saw him. She smiled, waved back and made her way over. Jacob saw inmates ogling her. He wanted to deck them.

Jacob greeted her with open arms, and they embraced. Once again, Sophia's hair smelled like roses. He held her tight and breathed her in.

"Thank you for coming," he said. "It's so good to see you."

"It's good to see you too."

As they sat down, she eyed his cast.

"What happened?"

He told her about being roughed up by Godzilla and airlifted to the hospital.

"It's a simple break," he said. "I should get my cast off in a couple of weeks."

Sophia's eyes welled with tears.

"It's okay," he said. "I'll be okay."

"I'm sorry," she said, wiping her eyes. "I worry about you in here."

"Please don't worry about me. I'll be fine. How are you?"

"I'm good."

"And Mateo?"

"He's good too. He's smart and sweet. Would you like to see his picture?"

"Sure."

She pulled her phone out of her small, white purse.

"Oh," she said, looking around. "I hope I'm allowed to have this in here."

"It's okay."

She leaned in and swiped through several photos.

"He has your eyes," Jacob said. "He's beautiful."

"Thank you."

"And he looks happy."

"He is."

"And how about you?"

"Well, being a single mom is hard, but raising Mateo is a joy. I can't imagine life without him."

She asked about his life in prison. He told her about his daily routine and Dawson. He also told her about being able to see Lake Michigan from the roof and how he hoped to buy a boat one day.

"That's very cool. I'd love to go out on it with you."

"I'll take you. And Mateo too."

She smiled.

"I'm learning some things in here," he said.

"Like what?"

"I realize I've made some bad choices in my life. Maybe it took being in here for me to see that. I want to make better choices."

"Maybe we both need to make better choices."

They held each other's gaze for a moment.

Jacob was probably the most decent person Sophia had ever known. How strange, she thought, that she would be meeting him in prison.

Jacob adored Sophia. That she was visiting him in prison was bittersweet. He hoped they would see each other after he got out.

"I think about you a lot," he said, surprising himself by disclosing such a private truth.

"And I think about you," she said with a smile.

What a relief, Jacob thought.

"Well, I guess I'd better get going," she said. "I told Mateo I'd take him to the park this afternoon."

"Thank you for coming," Jacob said, standing up.

She gave him a big hug and kissed him on the cheek.

"Take care of yourself," she said.

"I will."

He watched her walk away. Jacob wasn't sure if Sophia thought of him as more than a friend, but he knew he was in love with her.

CHAPTER NINETEEN

THE DAY after Jacob got his cast off, he went up on the roof to walk laps.

Bruno was shooting hoops. As Jacob walked by, he held up his right hand and smiled. Bruno saw his cast was gone.

"Ready for training?" he called out.

"Yeah," Jacob said with a nod.

"Good. We'll start tomorrow."

When Jacob got to the roof the following day, Bruno was already there, playing ball. As soon as he saw Jacob, he said, "Catch you guys later."

Bruno started walking toward the other end of the roof.

"Down here," he said.

Jacob didn't understand. There was only one basketball court, and Bruno didn't have a ball.

"Don't we need a ball?"

"Not yet. Let's sit."

Bruno sat on a bench against the wall. Jacob sat a few feet down.

"We'll work on your skills later," Bruno said. "First, let's talk."

"Okay."

"Let me ask you something. Why did you decide to play with us that day, the day you broke your arm?"

"What do you mean?"

"I mean why were you on the court?"

"Because you shamed me into it."

"I shamed you into it?"

"Yeah. You called me a punk."

"And you think that's a good reason to play ball?"

"I guess not."

"Look, playin up here ain't like shootin hoops on your driveway. This is street ball. It's rough. You're gonna get hurt. I can teach you some stuff, but you gotta want to play."

"I do want to play," Jacob said.

"Cool. Get up here early tomorrow. I'll show you a few things before the other guys start playin."

"Okay."

"See you tomorrow," Bruno said, getting up.

Bruno had surprised Jacob. He was expecting to work on passing and shooting that morning. But Bruno was right. Jacob had to really *want* to play before he could *learn* to play.

For most of his life, Jacob hadn't been clear or intentional about what he wanted. He'd fallen into activities like being online or making coffee without asking himself: is this really what I want?

Now he was sidelined, and the things he had done for so long were no longer available to him. *What do I really want?* Being with Sophia and piloting a boat on the open water came to mind.

Jacob leaned back against the prison wall and closed his eyes. He tried to imagine living a life beyond the things he had always done so mindlessly. He tried to imagine a life guided instead by his interests and desires, the things that called him, the things that lit him up.

CHAPTER TWENTY

AT LUNCH ONE DAY, Jacob sat across from Omar. They were the only ones left at the table.

Omar spoke without an accent. But he had coarse, black hair and olive skin and looked Middle Eastern. Jacob figured that's how he got his name.

"Dawson says you're a straight shooter," Omar said.

"He did?"

"Yeah. Can I ask you something?"

"Sure."

"I was wondering if you might have some advice for me."

"About what?"

"About what I should do when I get out of here."

Jacob was puzzled. Why would Omar come to him for advice on something like this?

"You know there are counselors here," Jacob said.

"I know, but I don't trust them."

"And you trust me?"

"Yeah, I do."

"Okay."

They went to a rec room and talked. Jacob learned Omar had a string of menial jobs, all of which he lost because he drank heavily and used drugs. He was high when a cop pulled him over one night. It was his second DUI. He was now serving a one-year sentence.

"How can I help?" Jacob said.

"When I get out, what do you think I should do?"

Jacob had never given anyone advice. He had no earthly idea what Omar should do. But he thought of a meeting he had with a counselor when he was in high school. He had asked Jacob a simple question, which he couldn't answer. Unsure of what else to say, he posed it for Omar.

"What are your interests?"

"I like to work on cars."

"So you want to be a mechanic?"

"Yeah, I guess. For starters anyway."

"For starters?"

"Well, I'd really like to own my own garage one day."

"Have you ever been a mechanic?"

"I've never had a *job* as a mechanic, if that's what you mean."

"Yeah."

"But I've worked on plenty of cars."

Jacob thought about what Omar had told him about losing jobs over the years. He knew Omar needed to get his act together but didn't want to hurt his feelings by coming right out and saying that.

"Well, I think you need to learn what it really means to be a mechanic," he said. "Get some experience. Show your employer what you can do, that you're reliable. After you've done that for a while, look around for openings at garages that need a manager."

"What if nobody will hire me as a manager? I'll be an ex-con. Who would put me in charge of anything?"

"Then open your own garage."

"But that would take money. I'm broke."

"You know, when I graduated from high school, I was broke too. But I got a job as a barista, making $16 an hour. Guess what? In three years, I saved $75,000, and I became a pretty good barista. Just focus on becoming a great mechanic and give it a little time. The money will follow."

"I hope so," Omar said.

"You got this."

"Thanks."

"You're welcome."

They shook hands, and Omar walked away. Jacob sat there, feeling surprised. Not just that he was able to offer helpful advice. But that anyone would come to him for advice. For the first time in his life, he felt valued.

When Jacob got back to his cell, Dawson was sitting on his bed, reading.

"I just talked with Omar," Jacob said.

As usual, Dawson said nothing.

"He told me it was your suggestion."

"That's right."

"Why?"

"Because you called bullshit."

"What?"

"Remember? You called bullshit on me."

"Yeah ..."

"Well, you pissed me off, but I've been thinking about what you said. You were right."

Dawson sounded almost conciliatory.

Jacob wondered if he'd gone too far.

"I didn't mean to hurt you," he said.

"Hurt me? You didn't hurt me, kid. You helped me. So I figured you might be able to help Omar too."

Dawson didn't thank Jacob. But after that, he started talking to him again and sitting next to him in the cafeteria again too.

Omar suggested Dax talk with Jacob. Dax also needed some advice about his options once he'd served his time.

As he did with Omar, Jacob mainly listened and helped Dax see where he needed to begin.

After that, Dax suggested another inmate talk with Jacob. Soon, Jacob was meeting with a new inmate about every week.

Jacob usually knew little or nothing about their areas of interest. But he was a good listener, and he surprised himself by having a knack for helping people think about ways to reach their dreams and especially how to get started.

Now he thought of his own dream of piloting a boat and what it would take to make that dream come true. It was one thing to yearn to be on the open water but quite another to buy a boat and learn to operate it.

So, in the prison library, he began reading about boating. He read every book and magazine the MCC library had on the subject.

He set his sights on a Bowrider Bayliner, a sleek powerboat recommended for beginners. He learned he could buy it from a dealer called Discover Boating in downtown Chicago. Through

Discover, he could also get training and take a test to get his license. They could also help him get insurance and a slip on a dock in the harbor.

But a new boat would cost $20,000. Where was he going to get that kind of money? His settlement with Jose Rivas had wiped out his savings.

Jacob thought about buying a used boat, which would cost a lot less. But then he realized he could get a job, save some money and get a loan. It was the kind of practical advice he was now used to giving his fellow inmates.

Besides, there was something about a new boat that fit with the new vision he was forming for his life. A used boat was about someone else's journey. Jacob was eager to begin a new journey of his own.

Living in a fantasy world and not paying attention to the real world was the reason Jacob was in prison. It was why Alicia Rivas would never see her husband and children again and they would never see her again. It was why Jacob had not yet grown up, even though he was technically an adult.

Now, at last, he was growing up. He was changing. There was something new. It was why he, who had never asserted himself, had challenged Henry Moyer, asked Jose Rivas to meet and called bullshit on Jack Dawson. It was why he had told Sophia he thinks about her all the time. It was why he was now helping his fellow inmates.

Jacob felt as though a new spirit was guiding him. In the past, he might have resisted such a spirit or not even noticed it. Now, though, he welcomed it.

. . .

That night, as Jacob was about to fall asleep, Emma came to mind. He wondered where she was. Was she finally in Heaven or still in Limbo?

Limbo had never really made sense to Jacob. How could God keep one of his children at a distance? And what had Emma ever done to deserve such a fate?

Jacob prayed Emma was with God and, if she wasn't, that the same spirit now guiding him might see her safely to the gate of Heaven.

CHAPTER TWENTY-ONE

IN A LETTER, Jacob told his parents about his meetings with his fellow inmates and what a difference they seemed to be making.

Hannah Novak was so impressed that she called Henry Moyer to let him know, hoping it might in some way help her son.

Jacob hadn't heard much from Moyer. He was surprised when he got a message that Moyer would be paying him a visit.

They met in a room designated for attorneys and their clients. Moyer was eager to learn more about the work Jacob had been doing with the other prisoners. He took notes.

"This might be very impressive to the parole board," he said. "Are you okay with me making them aware?"

"Sure. Do you really think it might help?"

"I don't want to get your hopes up, but it certainly can't hurt. I'll keep you posted."

.   .   .

Jacob and Sophia continued exchanging letters, and she now visited him every few weeks. Through these interactions, they revealed more and more about themselves.

Sophia shared how lonely she was. Her physical beauty had led boys, and eventually men, to take advantage of her. None of them loved her for who she really was, though. How ironic, she said, that someone who had gotten so much attention would feel so alone.

Jacob shared how he had lacked the confidence to face the real world. He told Sophia he was feeling self-confident for the first time in his life. How strange, he said, that he would have to be locked up to gain confidence.

Neither of them had shared these things with anyone else. Each of them began to appreciate the special bond between them. They didn't know where it would lead, but they looked forward to every letter and every visit.

Every morning for two weeks, Bruno had sacrificed his time playing basketball to give Jacob instruction on dribbling, shooting and passing.

Even more important, though, was what Bruno taught Jacob about protecting himself, mainly by paying attention to what was going on around him.

When Jacob was finally ready to get back in the game, the play was just as rough. Jacob still got bruises, and Godzilla was still there. But there were no more cheap shots.

When he'd served 23 months of his sentence, Jacob got his first phone call in prison. It was Henry Moyer.

"I have encouraging news," he said. "The parole board is

going to hear your case next month. There are no guarantees, of course. But I'm optimistic."

"Wow!" Jacob said. "That *is* great news."

"We'll need to do some prep," Moyer said.

They met the next day. Moyer went over the mechanics of how the parole hearing would work. He urged Jacob to reflect on what he'd learned from his experience, from the time he caused the accident that killed Alicia Rivas.

"This is what the parole board members will want to hear from you."

Jacob thought deeply about how this whole experience had changed him. He made notes and went over them with Moyer when they met again a week later.

"Perfect," Moyer said. "Now just keep your points brief and practice. You won't have much time. Naturally, you'll be nervous, and you don't want to miss a beat."

Jacob appeared before the parole board on a Thursday morning. It was made up of three men and two women. They were most interested in Jacob's work with the other inmates.

"So you've become a counselor of sorts?" one of the women asked.

"Yes."

"And what has this experience taught you?"

Jacob took a deep breath.

"I'd been living in my own world," he said. "I didn't really listen to anyone. What I'm learning is how important it is to listen. The men in here come to me and share their dreams. All I do is listen and help them decide where to begin to make those dreams come true. They thank me, but they've helped me as much as I've helped them. Maybe more. Through them,

I've learned I have something to offer the world, that I matter."

It wasn't exactly what he had planned to say, but he'd spoken from his heart. The board chair thanked Jacob for his time and told him they would be in touch.

He worried that he might have said either too much or too little. He hardly slept that night.

The following afternoon, he got a call from Moyer.

"I have great news," Moyer said.

After he hung up, Jacob leaned against the wall and began sobbing.

A few days before he was to be released, Jacob went up to the roof. It was mid-morning, and a guard was the only one there. Jacob walked over to one of the screened windows in the wall, looked out at the water and thought about his life.

Before prison, he had kept to himself. He had been living mainly in a virtual world. Now he was eager to venture out, to find his way in the real world.

He spotted a small boat in the harbor. He watched it circle then slowly make its way through the breakwalls and out into the Great Lake. Then he saw himself piloting that boat.

CHAPTER TWENTY-TWO

OVER TWO YEARS, Jacob had not only gotten to know a lot of inmates. He'd also made a lot of friends. How strange, he thought, that he had to be imprisoned to make friends.

They were all happy for him. There was no doubt some jealousy too, but that didn't keep his fellow inmates from wishing him well. In all, Jacob said goodbye to more than two dozen men. He promised to write them all.

Jacob found saying goodbye to Bruno especially hard. He owed him so much.

"How can I ever repay you?"

"You already have."

"What do you mean?"

"You taught me how to be a coach."

The two men embraced.

"Stay in touch," Bruno said, walking away.

"I will," Jacob called after him.

. . .

The morning of his release, a guard came to Jacob's cell and handed him his old clothes.

"I'll be back in 15 minutes," the guard said.

After two years of wearing a jumpsuit, it felt strange to put on normal clothes. Jacob's pants and shirt were now too big. Playing basketball had made him lean.

Dawson said nothing. He looked wistful. Jacob extended his hand, and Dawson took it.

"Thank you," Dawson said.

"I'm glad we were in here together," Jacob said.

Dawson opened his arms and gave him a hug.

Then Jack Dawson, who could not stop talking when they met, stepped back and nodded a silent goodbye.

Jacob's parents picked him up outside the prison gate. On the way home, they told him he was welcome to stay at home for as long as he'd like.

"I appreciate that," he said. "But just until I save enough to get my own place."

"Deal," his father said.

His mother made dinner that evening. Roast beef, mashed potatoes and green beans, with strawberry pie for dessert. Jacob's favorite.

"This is the best meal I've had in two years," he said.

"Is that a compliment?" his mother said with a little laugh.

After dinner, she brewed some decaf coffee, and the three of them took their mugs into the family room. Jacob's parents hadn't asked much about prison over dinner. He figured they didn't want to risk bringing up any unpleasant memories.

And he didn't volunteer much about his time in prison. He simply said, "I think it was good for me."

His father said, "So what are your plans?"

"I want to find a job. Eventually, I'd like to go to college. First, though, I want to save some money. And I'd like to buy a boat."

Jacob told his parents about looking out at Lake Michigan from the roof of the MCC, how he felt drawn to the water and how he had dreamed of owning a boat. But he wasn't sure how they would react to the idea of him buying something so expensive and non-essential when he would be living with them, presumably rent-free.

"What kind of boat do you have in mind?" his father said.

"A small powerboat. I've read about one that's ideal for beginners."

"That sounds interesting," his mother said, looking at Joe.

His father didn't say anything about the boat. Instead, he said, "What kind of job do you have in mind?"

Jacob knew this was his father's way of reminding him he needed to make money.

"Well, this might sound crazy," he said, "but I think I'd like to work in a coffee shop again."

"The Daily Grind?" his mother said.

"No. I felt like a robot there. I'm okay being a barista again, at least for a while. But I want to interact with people and work in a place that's part of the community."

"You should consider Portage Grounds," his mother said. "I stop there sometimes on my way to work. I know they're involved in the community. Good coffee too."

"Thanks," Jacob said. "I think I'll go over there tomorrow."

"You're going to need a phone again," she said. "I'll be happy to take you out to get one."

"We'll spot you," his father said.

"Thanks. That'd be great."

"We still have our landline phone too," his mother said.

Jacob's eyes lit up.

"If you wouldn't mind, I'd like to make a call."

"Feel free," his mother said.

His parents got up.

"We both have early mornings," his mother said. "If it's okay, we'll say good night."

"Sure," Jacob said. "I'm used to getting to bed early too."

He gave them both a hug and kissed his mother on the cheek.

"Welcome home," they said.

Jacob sensed his parents weren't keen about him buying a boat, at least not now. That bothered him a little, but he would deal with it later. Now he sat back down and called Sophia. He hoped he wasn't calling too late.

"Hello?"

"Sophia, it's Jacob. I'm out. I'm calling you from my parents' house."

"Jacob! How great to hear your voice."

"How are you?"

"I'm fine. I'd love to see you. Would you like to come over and have dinner with us tomorrow?"

"I'd love to."

"Great. I'll make enchiladas. I hope that sounds okay."

"That sounds wonderful."

"Oh, do you need a ride? I'd be happy to pick you up."

"Thanks, but I'll manage it."

"Cool. Does 6:00 sound okay?"

"Perfect."

"Great. We'll see you then. I can't wait for you to meet Mateo."

"And I can't wait to meet him — and see you."

. . .

Jacob turned out the lights and went upstairs. He used to think his bedroom was small, but after being cooped up in a tiny cell for two years, it now seemed spacious.

He decided to take a shower. What a luxury to have a shower to himself.

Back in his room, Jacob noticed his old laptop was still on his desk. His TV was still on his dresser too. He was tempted to grab the remote, but he wanted to stay unplugged a little longer.

He turned off his lamp and slipped into bed.

I made it, he thought. Not only that, but the experience he had dreaded had reshaped him and given him a new direction. Now he was eager to begin anew.

CHAPTER TWENTY-THREE

WHEN JACOB AWOKE in the morning, his parents had already left for work. His mother had left a note on the kitchen counter.

Good morning, Jacob. Enjoy your day. Love, Mom

After breakfast, Jacob brushed his teeth, shaved and got dressed. His clothes were all a little loose now. Maybe his mother could take him shopping for some new clothes when they went out to buy a cell phone.

He headed out on foot to Portage Grounds, less than a mile away. It was a modern brick building, set back from Irving Park Road, the main road through Portage Park.

There was a patio area out front, with aluminum tables and chairs, bright yellow umbrellas and stone planters filled with flowers. It was a warm, sunny morning, and people were having breakfast out there.

Stepping inside, Jacob saw a sign that read:

Working at The Daily Grind, Jacob had thought coffee was coffee and all businesses were alike. The idea that a coffee shop could be more than a place that dispensed coffee and warmed up frozen breakfast sandwiches piqued his interest.

He looked around. The place was spacious and spotless but cozy, with armchairs, a sofa and a fireplace. Soft music filled the air, and floor-to-ceiling windows let in lots of sunlight. What a contrast with the dark, grimey, noisy MCC chow hall.

Jacob got in line. Looking up at the menu board, he was impressed by the range of freshly made pastries and kolaches.

Stepping up to the counter, Jacob ordered a tall latte and asked if he could speak with the manager.

"That's me," his server said with a smile.

Her name tag said Isabella. She was young, with dark skin and long, dark hair pulled back in a ponytail. She spoke with a Spanish accent.

"Good morning. My name is Jacob Novak."

"Hi, Jacob. I'm Isabella Garcia. How can I help you?"

"I was wondering if you're hiring."

"Yes, we are. Are you interested?"

"Yes."

"What kind of a position are you looking for?"

"Well, I was a barista in my most recent job."

"I'd be happy to talk with you. Mornings are our busiest

time, as you can see. Can you come back this afternoon, say around 3:00?"

"That sounds great. I'll see you then. By the way, please call me Izzy."

"Thanks, Izzy. I'll see you this afternoon."

At 2:30, Jacob set out for Portage Grounds. He'd driven this way countless times, but this was only the second time he'd walked it.

This time, he cut through Portage Park, the namesake of his town. He'd nearly forgotten about the park. His parents used to take him there when he was a boy.

Now as he walked through the park, Jacob was mindful of the Earth beneath his feet, the fragrance of wildflowers and the laughter of children: the feel, the smell, the sound of the real world.

He had missed these things. He had missed living in the real world, and he hoped he would never lose touch with it again.

Jacob met with Izzy promptly at three. They sat at a table near a back window, overlooking a garden with ornamental grasses, small trees and flowers.

Right up front, Jacob told her he'd just spent two years in prison.

"Oh?"

He told her why he was there, how the experience had changed him and that he was looking for a job that would enable him to save for college.

"But not just any job," he said. "I want to make a difference."

"I see," she said. "We're all about making a difference in this community. We source our food from local farmers. Ten percent of our profits goes to support local greenbelt projects. We make our conference room available free to local groups that need a place to meet. Of course, people come here for great coffee and food. But everyone who works here knows our job doesn't stop there."

"That's very cool," he said. "I'd love to be a part of a place like this."

"Well, I'm glad you're interested, and I appreciate you coming in this afternoon. I'll get back to you tomorrow. Okay?"

"Great."

"Will you be stopping in for coffee in the morning?"

"Yes."

"Cool. I'll let you know then."

"Thank you."

Walking home, Jacob wondered why Izzy needed more time. Was she concerned about his being an ex-con?

But then he realized that, if she was concerned, there was nothing he could do about it. After all, he *was* an ex-con.

But Jacob also knew he was much more than that, and whether it was at Portage Grounds or somewhere else, he was going to find his place in the world, and he *was* going to make a difference. His days of sitting on the sidelines were over.

CHAPTER TWENTY-FOUR

SOPHIA LIVED in an apartment building in Old Irving. It was about a mile and a half from Jacob's house, a straight shot across Irving Park Road.

Jacob decided to walk to Sophia's place and Uber home. He didn't want to inconvenience Sophia or have his parents drive him, like he was a kid.

He left the house a little before 5:00. His parents still weren't home, so he left them a note. He mentioned his interview at Portage Grounds.

"Fingers crossed," he wrote.

He walked on the sidewalk along Irving Park. When he got to North Cicero Avenue, he stopped. It was the site of his crash.

Now he was at a new crossroads. His future was uncertain, but he wasn't going to let that uncertainty hold him back.

He watched the light change, then he made his way across the intersection where he'd nearly been destroyed. This time, he paid attention to everything around him. Bruno would be proud, he thought.

His parents had given him $100 for incidentals. He stopped at a florist. He wanted to bring Sophia a gift and thought she might like flowers. But as he looked around at the bouquets, they seemed excessive. Instead, he had the florist wrap a single red rose in white tissue paper.

As he was about to pay, Jacob noticed a hodgepodge of knick knacks on the top of a display case. He spotted a Matchbox car, a red Corvette. He had one just like it as a kid and thought Mateo might like it too. He picked it up and handed it to the florist.

"This too, please."

He had her put it in a small bag.

Jacob arrived in the lobby of Sophia's apartment building about 5:45. Waiting for her, Jacob felt a little like he had the first time Sophia had come over to his table at lunch in kindergarten. He had butterflies in his stomach.

At 6:00, the elevator doors opened, and out walked Sophia, smiling and holding her son's hand. She wore blue jeans, a pink sweatshirt and white tennis shoes. She made casual look elegant.

"Jacob!" she said, hurrying over and giving him a warm embrace.

He held her for a long moment. Once again, her hair smelled like roses.

"Welcome," she whispered in his ear.

They stepped back from one another, and he handed her the rose.

"How thoughtful. Thank you."

Then she said, "Jacob, this is Mateo."

The boy looked up at Jacob with big, brown eyes that

reminded him of Sophia's the day they met.

"Hello, Mateo. I brought something for you too."

Jacob handed Mateo the bag. He wasn't sure what to do.

"Open it," Sophia said.

Mateo opened the bag, looked inside and said, "Wow!"

He reached in and pulled out the little car.

"Look!" he said to his mother, holding it up.

"How cool," she said.

Then, looking at Jacob, she said, "Thank you."

Sophia was struck by Jacob's kindness. His gifts were small and simple but thoughtful. But no one had ever given her a single rose.

She was used to guys hitting on her, but Jacob was different. He had always been different. He had always seemed happy just to be with her. Maybe I needed to grow up to appreciate that, she thought.

"Hungry?" she said.

"Starving."

"Well, dinner is almost ready. Let's go up."

Their apartment, on the second floor, was small and neat. Sophia put her rose in a slender vase, which she placed in the center of a small, round table in the main room near the kitchen.

"Dinner will be ready in a few minutes," she said. "Why don't you two have a seat in the family room?"

Mateo hitched himself up on the sofa, and Jacob sunk into an upholstered armchair. Even after two days with his parents, he was still getting used to cushioned chairs again.

"Mommy showed me your picture," Mateo said. "You look different."

Sophia laughed.

"That's because he was in high school," she said. "People change."

It warmed Jacob's heart to think Sophia had a picture of him and that she'd shown her son.

"So I understand you're in kindergarten," Jacob said.

"Yes."

"Do you like it?"

"I love it."

"That's great. What do you like most about it?"

"Art class. I like to draw."

"What do you like to draw?"

"All kinds of things. Want to see my drawings?"

"I'd love to."

"I'll be right back."

Mateo got up and ran into another room.

"He wants to be an artist," Sophia said from the kitchen.

"Imagine that," Jacob said with a smile.

Mateo returned with a sketchbook and a blue pencil pouch. He put the sketchbook on the coffee table and opened it. Jacob came over and sat on the sofa so he could see.

"This is a house," Mateo said.

"That's a cool-looking house."

"Mom and I are going to live in a house like this one day."

He flipped the page. There was a hillside covered with flowers.

"Beautiful," Jacob said.

Mateo smiled. He kept turning pages, revealing his drawings of a diverse assortment of people, places and things.

"Mateo, these are really good," Jacob said. "You're quite an artist."

"Thank you. Would you like me to draw something for you?"

"I'd love that."

"What would you like me to draw?"

"Hmmm. How about a guy in a boat on a lake?"

"A big lake?"

"Yeah."

Mateo's eyes lit up.

"I think I can do that!"

Jacob looked over at Sophia. She was standing in the kitchen, watching them. She looked happy.

"Time for dinner, guys," she said.

Over dinner, they talked mainly about Mateo. He shared openly and laughed easily. He wasn't the least bit shy. He's so different from me at that age, Jacob thought.

After dinner, Jacob helped Sophia clean up the kitchen as Mateo resumed drawing in his sketchbook in the family room.

"You're so good with him," she said.

"He's a great kid. And he draws like you did when you were a kid."

"You remember?"

"How could I forget? I was your student."

She laughed.

They went into the family room and sat down on the sofa.

"Look what I drew, Jacob!" Mateo said, holding up his sketchbook.

It was a drawing of a man in a white boat in blue water that spanned the page. In the light blue sky were clouds, birds and the sun.

"That's fantastic!" Jacob said.

"Yes," said Sophia. "It's really good."

"Thanks," Mateo said.

He turned the page and kept drawing as Sophia and Jacob chatted.

At 8:00, she said, "All right, Mateo. Time to get ready for bed."

"I should go," Jacob said.

"Don't go. I'd love to catch up."

"Okay."

"Good night, Mateo," Jacob said. "I hope to see you again soon."

"Good night, Jacob."

With his sketchbook under his arm and his pencil pouch in hand, Mateo scampered to his bedroom. Sophia followed him.

"I'll be right back," she said.

About 10 minutes later, she returned.

"Would you like something to drink?"

"I'd love a glass of wine, if you'd join me."

"Is red okay?"

"Perfect."

She poured two glasses. She handed him one, then sat back down and slipped off her shoes.

"To new beginnings," she said, raising her glass.

"To new beginnings."

Jacob watched Sophia sip her wine. He could hardly believe he was sitting right next to her. He'd dreamed of a moment like this.

"I hope the last two years haven't been too hard for you," she said.

"You know, I think being in prison was actually good for me."

"How so?"

"Before I went to prison, I felt like I didn't matter. But when I got in there, and guys started coming to me for advice, I felt like I really had something to offer."

"You do matter," she said softly.

He marveled at her. She had a way of speaking to him unlike anyone else. She seemed to know his heart and really care about him. He had felt that from the day they met.

"And how about you?" he said. "How are you doing?"

"I'm okay. As you can see, Mateo is doing great. I'm glad he's growing up in a place where he feels loved. Being a single mom is hard, but I know we're much better off than if I had stayed with Matt."

"You're a wonderful mother. You can be very proud."

"Thank you."

She sipped her wine.

"So what will you do now?" she said.

Jacob told her about his interview at Portage Grounds and that he wanted to save for college.

"I'm not sure what I'll study, but I know having a degree will open some new doors for me. In the meantime, I'm going to buy a boat."

"A boat? What kind of boat?"

"A small powerboat. It's called a Bayliner. I'm going to learn how to operate it and get a license. I'll dock it in the Chicago Harbor."

"Wow! What made you decide to get a boat?"

"I've always been drawn to the water. From the roof of the MCC, I could see the Chicago Harbor and Lake Michigan. Watching all the boats made me want to get one of my own."

"That's so cool."

He sat quietly for a moment and studied her face. There was something else he wanted to tell her, but he hesitated.

"What?" she said.

"Before I went to prison, I was hanging back. I was stuck. But I'm tired of hanging back. I want to get into the real world.

I know it might sound strange, but somehow taking a boat out on the open water fits with that."

"It doesn't sound strange at all. I'm happy for you. I'm glad you're breaking free."

She had finished her wine.

"Would you like another glass?" she said.

He wanted to say yes, but he didn't want to overstay.

"No, thanks. I'd better get going."

"Okay."

"Can I use your phone to call an Uber?"

"No worries. I've got the app."

She grabbed her phone from the coffee table.

He grabbed his wallet and pulled out a credit card. His father had given him one of his until he got a new one of his own.

"Here," he said, handing it to her. "Use this."

"Okay."

A minute later, she said, "All set," handing the card back. "Your driver is five minutes away."

They got up, and Sophia put their wine glasses on the kitchen counter.

Walking Jacob to the door, she said, "I'm off work next Tuesday. Mateo has school. Would you like to get together?"

"Sure."

"I don't know if you'd be interested, but there's a new exhibit at the Art Institute I'd really like to see."

"I'd love that."

"Cool. Maybe we could go in the morning and have lunch in the cafe there."

"That sounds great."

Then he remembered Portage Grounds.

"Oh, I just remembered. I might be working by then."

"That's okay. We can make it another time."

"No, if I get the job, I'll just let them know I need to be off next Tuesday."

She smiled.

"I can pick you up," she said.

"That'd be great."

"9:30?"

"Perfect."

They stood at the door, face to face. Just as he was about to give her a hug, she put her arms around his neck, reached up and kissed him on the lips. It wasn't a long kiss. It didn't have to be. A kiss like that meant he was more than just a friend.

"Good night," she said, just above a whisper, looking into his eyes.

When he got out to the street, Jacob's ride was waiting. Ten minutes later, he was home. On the way, he hadn't said a word. He'd been thinking about that kiss.

In the morning, Jacob walked to Portland Grounds. It was crowded. He saw that Izzy was working the counter again and got in line. She saw him and smiled. He hoped that was a good sign.

When he got to the counter, she said, "I'd love for you to come work with us. You'd start at $17 an hour."

Jacob accepted on the spot.

"Great," she said. "If you come back at 3:00 again, we'll go over everything."

"Thanks," he said, shaking her hand. "I'll see you then."

He was about to leave when he remembered to order a tall latte to go.

. . .

As soon as he got home, Jacob called Sophia.

"I'm thrilled for you," she said. "Let's celebrate next Tuesday."

It felt so good to be able to share his good news with Sophia. He couldn't wait to tell his parents too. He decided to make them dinner to celebrate and give something back.

Walking to a grocery store, Jacob was amazed by the freedom he now had. It made him think of the guys at the MCC. He'd promised to write them. After he bought food, Jacob stopped at a gift shop and bought two boxes of blank note cards.

Back home, he made marinara sauce and meatballs. Spaghetti and meatballs was one of the few dishes Jacob had mastered.

When the sauce was on the stove and the meatballs were in the oven, he sat at the kitchen table and began writing notes to his friends at the MCC. Over the course of a couple of hours, he wrote more than a dozen. They were all notes of encouragement.

The meatballs were now marinating in the sauce, and a sweet, spicy aroma filled the air. He hoped his parents would be pleasantly surprised when they got home.

Shortly after two, Jacob turned off the stove and took off for Portage Grounds. It would take him only 15 minutes to get there. But this time, he wanted to sit for a little while on a bench in the park to pause for a moment and say a prayer of thanksgiving.

CHAPTER TWENTY-FIVE

IN THE MORNING, Jacob rose with the sun. For two years, he had awoken in half-light. He didn't realize how much he missed the rising sun.

Once again, his parents had already left for work. Over breakfast, Jacob finished writing notes to his friends at the MCC. He also wrote Sophia a thank-you note for dinner.

Then he walked to the post office, where he bought two books of stamps and mailed the cards, more than 20 in all.

Jacob would start work at Portage Grounds the following morning. His mother was going to take him to the Apple store in Lincoln Park to buy a phone that evening. He definitely needed a phone, but he made a vow to himself that he would use it sparingly. Before he went to prison, he would spend hours at a time on his phone, doomscrolling.

Now that he had a job, Jacob started thinking about that boat again. He'd seen ads for it in magazines in the MCC library but hadn't checked it out online. He hadn't *been* online for two years.

He went up to his room, plugged in his old laptop and pressed the on button. The white Apple logo appeared like a phantom. He couldn't remember his password, so he reset it. His screen lit up, and all his old icons reemerged along the bottom.

He typed in Discover Boating Chicago, and the website popped up. A video montage featuring happy-looking people in sleek boats speeding across turquoise water filled his screen. He clicked through to "Bayliner." Images of the most popular models flashed up. He hadn't realized there were so many options.

He clicked on a boat checklist tab. There he found all the steps involved in buying a new boat: picking a model, selecting colors and features, getting a loan, securing registration, taking a test to get a license, buying insurance and arranging for towing and docking.

It was all a bit overwhelming. Jacob sat back and tried to think about all these steps in order, as a process. He was following the advice he had given his fellow inmates.

To start, he needed to go to the dealership, which was in the Wintrust Building, downtown. He hoped his father could take him on Sunday, a day off work for both of them.

Jacob leaned forward and clicked back to the Discover Boating home page. He again watched the videos of people boating. Then he closed his eyes and envisioned himself piloting a boat on the open water.

In his vision, someone was sitting next to him. He looked over and saw Sophia, smiling and radiant, the wind tousling her dark brown hair. *I'm going to make that dream come true.*

. . .

That evening, Jacob's mother took him out to shop for a phone and new clothes.

In the car, he said, "Mom, can I ask you something?"

"Sure."

"It's about Emma."

His mother looked straight ahead and said nothing.

"Do you think she's still in Limbo?"

"I don't know."

"Do you believe in Limbo?"

"Yes."

"Why?"

"That's what we were taught in school."

"But does it make any sense to you? I mean how could a baby *not* go to Heaven?"

"Emma wasn't baptized," his mother said, her voice breaking.

"I'm sorry, Mom. I didn't mean to upset you."

"It's okay," she said, clearing her throat.

Silence.

"What do *you* think?" his mother said.

"I think Emma's with God."

She reached over and put her hand on his.

"I'm beginning to think you're right," she said.

CHAPTER TWENTY-SIX

WHEN IT CAME to making coffee drinks, Jacob was out of practice. But it all came back fast.

Unlike at The Daily Grind, though, his responsibilities at Portage Grounds went far beyond being a barista. Now he had to also work the counter and the drive-thru, clean tables and restrooms, wash dishes, take out garbage, help in the kitchen and water the outdoor plants. Izzy had told him every team member is expected to "wear many hats" and work hard.

The biggest change, though, was waiting on customers.

For most of his life, Jacob had avoided conversations with strangers. But his most recent experiences, especially with the MCC inmates, had changed him. Now he enjoyed talking with people.

It showed. He was friendly. People liked being around him. A couple of his female co-workers even flirted with him. Jacob liked the attention, but he was interested in only one woman. He smiled but didn't flirt back.

On the afternoon of his third day at work, Jacob spotted an

older man sitting alone at a table in the corner. He was shabbily dressed. At first glance, he looked like an older version of Omar, with gray in his coarse black hair.

The man sat with his hands folded on the table and looked out the window. He had nothing with him, not even a phone. Once in a while, he would glance over at the counter. Jacob got the sense he was looking at him.

When there was no one in line and the team had caught up on orders, Jacob decided to walk over.

"Good afternoon," he said.

"Hello."

"May I offer you something?"

"I don't ... I don't have any money."

"That's okay."

"Are you sure?"

"Yeah. I'll be right back."

Back behind the counter, Jacob opened his wallet, pulled out a $10 bill and put it on the register. He poured a mug of coffee and set it on a tray. He grabbed a blueberry muffin, packets of creamer and sugar, napkins and a stir stick and placed them on the tray too. Then he walked over and gently placed the tray on the table.

The man looked at all the items on the tray, then up at Jacob.

"Thank you," he said.

"Enjoy."

Jacob got back to work. When no one was in line, Izzy approached him.

"May I see you for a minute?" she said.

"Sure."

Izzy looked serious. Jacob sensed he was in trouble. He followed her to the conference room and stepped inside.

"I saw what you did," she said.

"He looked hungry."

She smiled and shook her head.

"I'm not mad at you, Jacob. I'm proud of you, and I want to commend you for bringing what we stand for here to life."

Jacob was stunned.

"Now," she said with a grin, "we're not running a charity. But I know you'll use your good judgment."

"Yeah, I will."

"I know you will. I'm glad you're on our team."

Back behind the counter, Jacob looked over at the man in the corner. He was cradling the coffee mug in his hands. Seeing Jacob look his way, he smiled — and looked even more like Omar.

On Sunday, Jacob's father drove him to Discover Boating.

On the way, his father said, "I have to tell you I wasn't sure about your buying a boat when you first mentioned it."

"I could tell."

"But I'm okay with it now."

"What changed your mind? When I got a job?"

"No. I thought about my father and how he reacted when I decided to go my own way, after high school. He gave me a hard time. He made me feel bad. I made a vow to myself long ago, before you were born, that I wouldn't treat my children that way. We make choices, Jacob. You made a bad choice the night you caused that accident. But you learned from it, and you're making better choices now. Life isn't about being perfect. It's about learning from our mistakes and improving. That's what you're doing, and I'm proud of you."

Jacob's father was a man of few words, and he didn't show

his emotions easily. This was the most he had ever said to Jacob at one time. In that moment, Jacob felt deeply grateful to be his father's son. He hoped he would be such a good father one day.

"Thanks, Dad."

Then he added, "I love you."

"I love you too," his father said, looking ahead at the road.

A portly, middle-aged salesman named Bob led them to the Bayliner models. Jacob really liked the look of the Element M17. He'd seen it online. It was exactly the boat he had in mind.

The price wasn't posted.

"How much is this one?" Jacob said, hoping it was on sale.

"This one starts at $21,000," Bob said. "We do offer financing."

"What's your loan rate?" Jacob's father said.

"Six percent."

"On the whole amount?"

"Yes."

Jacob looked at his father.

"That's fair," he said.

Bob went over the features of the boat, including all the options and upgrades. He was clearly trying to upsell. But the only option Jacob was interested in was the color of the hull. He wanted it to be white with a marine blue stripe wrapped around the top.

"We can do that," Bob said.

"I'd also like to have the name of the boat painted near the stern, on both sides, and on the transom," Jacob said.

"Sure, we can do that too. What name would you like?"

"Liberation," Jacob said, looking at his father.

His father smiled and nodded.

"If I financed the whole thing, what would my monthly payment be?" Jacob said.

"About $200," Bob said.

"I'd be happy to co-sign for the loan," said Jacob's father.

"That's very generous, Mr. Novak, and it's certainly up to you," Bob said. "But as long as Jacob is good for the monthly payment, that won't be necessary."

"Thanks, Dad," Jacob said. "I do think I can cover it."

"Okay."

"Well, would you like to make a purchase today?" Bob said.

"Yes," said Jacob, barely able to contain his excitement.

On the way home, Jacob told his father renting a slip in the harbor would run about $500 a year.

"That sounds reasonable."

"Yeah, but I don't have the money, at least not yet."

"Do you want me to cover it?"

"Would you? I'll pay you back."

"No need. Consider it a gift from Mom and me. A home-coming gift."

CHAPTER TWENTY-SEVEN

ON TUESDAY, Jacob and Sophia had a wonderful time at the Art Institute. He knew little about art. She loved it. When they were kids, Sophia wanted to be an artist. She had no formal training, but she became a student of art. As they walked through the exhibits, Sophia eagerly offered her perspective.

Jacob was very happy to be her art student once again.

Over lunch, Jacob told Sophia about the new boat he had ordered, including what he'd chosen to name it.

"Good choice," she said.

She watched Jacob as he ate. He was not so different from the boy she had met so long ago. There was a goodness about him. That hadn't changed. It was his goodness that drew her to him in the first place. It drew her to him still.

But there was something more. Sitting this close, with sunlight streaming through the large windows, she noticed the red in his sandy blond hair. She hadn't noticed that before. Or the splash of amber in his green eyes. Or how toned he had become.

Sophia had always thought of Jacob as a friend. Now she found herself strongly attracted to him and thinking of him as more than a friend.

Jacob sensed there was something different in the way Sophia was looking at him.

"Is everything okay?" he said, inexperienced as he was in the art of romance.

"Yes," she said, blushing a little. "Fine."

"Good," he said with a smile.

"You're a good man, Jacob," she said, sliding her hand across the table and touching his arm.

"Thank you."

After lunch, Sophia took Jacob home. His parents were at work.

"Would you like to come in?" he said.

She was burning to say yes, but she had to pick up Mateo at school.

"I'd love to, but I need to get going. I'm sorry."

"I understand. I had a great time. And thanks for the ride."

He leaned over to give Sophia a hug, but she put her hands on the sides of his face and kissed him on the lips. This time, it was a longer kiss. Between the softness of her lips and the brush of her hair on his face, Jacob had to tear himself away.

"See you soon," she called after him.

"Yeah," he said, feeling a little dizzy.

That Sunday, Jacob and Sophia took Mateo to the Chicago Children's Museum. He painted in the art studio there all afternoon.

Afterwards, they went back to Sophia's place. She had

invited Jacob to join them for dinner. Sophia made pepian, a chicken stew with veggies and rice.

"It's the national dish in Guatemala," she said.

She was always expanding his world.

After dinner, Mateo got out his art supplies and went to work in the family room. A little while later, he showed Sophia and Jacob a picture he'd drawn and colored. It featured a woman, a man and a boy, standing side by side, holding hands.

"It's us," Mateo said proudly.

"That's really good," Sophia said.

He'd printed Mateo and Mom under their likenesses, but there was no name under the drawing of Jacob.

"I didn't know how to spell your name," the boy said sheepishly.

"Would you like me to spell it?"

"Yes, please," Mateo said, grabbing a red crayon.

Jacob said the letters slowly, and Mateo wrote them down. When he was finished, he stared at Jacob's name, as if he were trying to memorize the spelling.

"Good job," Jacob said. "Now your picture is complete."

When he was in prison, Jacob wondered if he would ever be a father, and he worried about whether he could ever be a good role model for a child. Now, knowing his presence in Mateo's life had led him to create something so beautiful, that old worry fell away.

When it was Mateo's bedtime, he said good night to Jacob and gave him a hug. As Sophia followed her son to his bedroom, she turned to Jacob and said, "I'll be right back."

When she got back, Jacob was standing near the door. He had already called an Uber.

Sophia walked over and said, "Would you like to spend the night?"

Jacob was floored. He wanted so badly to say yes, but he thought of Mateo. What would he think if he saw Jacob there in the morning? He felt he should talk about that with Sophia first, but now didn't seem the time.

He took her hands.

"I'd love to, but not tonight. Soon, though. Okay?"

"Yes," she said with a smile.

She reached up, put her arms around Jacob's neck and kissed him lovingly.

On his ride home, Jacob thought about Sophia asking him to spend the night — and him saying no.

Am I nuts?

CHAPTER TWENTY-EIGHT

JACOB ASKED Izzy for a day off. She said yes and didn't ask why. If she had, he would have told her he needed to get some things in order. He would have been telling the truth.

At his sentencing hearing, Jacob had made peace with Jose Rivas. But he felt a need to make peace with Alicia Rivas too. Ever since he learned of her death, she was never far from his thoughts.

Soon after he'd been released from prison and moved back home, Jacob went online and found her obituary. He learned she'd been buried at St. Adalbert Cemetery in Niles, about five miles north of his house.

After his parents had left for work, Jacob called an Uber. On his ride to the cemetery, he spotted a Prius and thought of his accident. Seeing a Prius just then felt eerie.

The driver dropped Jacob at the cemetery office. Stepping inside, he saw an older woman sitting behind a desk.

"May I help you, young man?" she said.

"Good morning. Can you please direct me to the gravesite of Alicia Rivas?"

"Certainly. Let me locate it for you," she said, typing on her computer keyboard. "Here it is. Ms. Rivas' grave is on Saint Anne's Way. It's not far from here. Let me show you."

She picked up a map and drew a circle around the site.

"Right there," she said, handing him the map.

"Just head up this drive," she said, swiveling in her chair and pointing to a window, "and take the first right. That's Saint Anne's Way. Ms. Rivas' grave will be about midway down on the left."

"Thank you."

"Is there anything else I can help you with?"

"Yes. Can you tell me where I can find the gravesite for Emma Novak?"

She turned back to her computer, and her fingers skipped over the keyboard.

"Ms. Novak's gravesite is on Saint Christopher. Saint Anne's Way runs right into it. Take a left at Saint Christopher, and you'll see the gravesite about 50 yards down on your right. If you like, I can mark it on your map."

"That's okay. I'll remember. Thank you."

Jacob walked out and followed the drive behind the cemetery office. It was a warm, bright morning, and the sun felt good. Birds chirped, and a lawnmower hummed in the distance.

He could tell from the dates on the gravestones and the size of the trees that this was an old cemetery. The oaks, sycamores and cedars stood like sentinels, and the gently rolling hills evoked a certain serenity.

Jacob checked the map and took a right at Saint Anne's Way. About midway, he stepped into the grass and carefully made his way through rows of gravestones. He looked for Rivas but didn't see it.

Then he began looking down at the smaller, flat headstones. Soon he came upon the one he was looking for. Within its rough stone edges was a finely polished rectangle. In the center was etched Alicia Rivas, 1980 - 2021.

Jacob folded his hands in front of him and looked down at the small stone with its simple marking.

So she was only 41 years old. He had robbed her of decades of life. He had paid for his crime, but how could he ever make things right for this woman and her family?

I can't.

Jacob knelt down in the grass, which was still damp with dew. He folded his hands in prayer, as he used to in church, and closed his eyes.

"I'm sorry, Mrs. Rivas," he said in a low voice. "I can't undo what I've done. But I can tell you I will pay attention, pay attention to others, pay attention to the world. You did not die in vain. I hope we'll meet one day. Until then, I wish you peace, and I pray you can forgive me."

A warm breeze caressed his face. He felt something, someone. He opened his eyes, half expecting to see someone there. But there was only the tombstone.

Jacob looked around. Everything was still. He thought of Jose Rivas saying "I forgive you" as he headed off to prison. He remembered the sense of peace that had given him. He had that same feeling now.

He got up, walked back to the road and headed for his sister's grave. He found it not far from Saint Christopher. Her tombstone was also small and flat. In it was etched Emma Novak, 2002.

Again, Jacob knelt down, folded his hands and closed his eyes.

"Emma, it's me," he said in a loud whisper, "your brother. I'm sorry we didn't get to know each other. Mom says you might be in Limbo, but I think you're in Heaven. Wherever you are, please pray for me and Mom and Dad too. They miss you so much. I know we'll all be together again. I'll hold you and kiss you then."

On his ride home, Jacob reflected on his experience that morning. He had gone to the cemetery to make peace with Alicia Rivas. He felt he had done that.

In the process, he felt even more resolved to pay attention to others and break free of the lonely world that had imprisoned him for so long. He wanted to be there for people like the inmates he had befriended, the old man in Portage Grounds and Sophia and Mateo.

Jacob didn't know what lay ahead for him, but for the first time in his life, he felt he was on the right path.

CHAPTER TWENTY-NINE

JACOB ACED the online test for his boating license and applied for a slip in the Chicago Harbor. He had already registered his new boat, and it would be ready for delivery soon.

He was making a tall latte at work when his phone rang. *Discover Boating* popped up on the screen. It was Bob, letting him know his boat was all ready to go.

On his break, Jacob texted Sophia to share his good news.

She bounced right back.

> So happy for you. Can't wait to take a
> ride!

A few days later, the harbor office called. His application had been approved, and his slip had been assigned. He just needed to come in and sign a few papers.

After work, his father took Jacob downtown, and he signed for the slip. As promised, his father covered the cost.

On the way home, Jacob called Bob. He told him he now had a slip and asked when Discover could deliver his boat.

"We can have it there tomorrow."

Tomorrow was Friday. It was a work day, but Jacob knew Izzy would let him off a little early.

"How about 4:00?" he said.

"Sounds good," said Bob. "I'll have a guy meet you at the dock then."

"Great."

Jacob's father overheard the conversation.

"I don't think I can get off work tomorrow in time to get you down to the harbor by four," he said.

"It's okay, Dad. I'll find my own transportation this time. Thanks."

The next day, Jacob clocked out at 3:00. He called an Uber to pick him up at Portage Grounds. It would cost him $20 each way. For Jacob, that was real money, but it felt right to make this particular trip by himself.

He got to the harbor in time to greet the driver and watch him put his new boat in the water and maneuver it into his slip.

"Gassed up and ready to go," he said, handing Jacob the keys and a thin stack of papers sealed in plastic. "Enjoy."

"Thanks," Jacob said, handing him a ten.

After the driver left, Jacob stood on the dock and looked down at his boat for a long time. *His* boat. It was hard to believe.

She was gorgeous, sleek and white with a blue-striped hull, a low-slung windshield and an open bow with cushioned seats. There were two, white swivel seats in the graphite-colored cockpit, with the captain's seat on the starboard side.

But as cool as all these features were, the one that really stood out for Jacob was the name of the boat. *Liberation.*

Looking at it now, he thought of his own liberation. Not just being released from prison but from all that had confined him for so long. At last, he was breaking free.

The sun was getting low. Jacob was eager to take his new boat out for a short ride, but he hesitated. *What if I cause an accident? Would my parole be revoked? Should I take lessons with an experienced pilot?*

Jacob thought of the first time he'd tried to play basketball at the MCC. He ended up in the hospital. But then he thought of what Bruno had taught him: to make sure he really wanted to play, that he had the skills to play and to pay attention to what was going on around him.

I've wanted to have my own boat and take it out on the water for a long time. I've trained for this. I'll pay close attention to what's going on around me.

I'm going for it.

He unwound the ropes from the metal cleats on the dock, grabbed hold of the frame of the windshield and stepped on board. The boat gently rocked, and he steadied himself. Sitting in the captain's seat, he looked over the dashboard and inserted the key. He turned it, and the engine rumbled to life.

The boat, now floating free, was pointed toward the harbor. He pushed the throttle lever forward slightly, and she slowly moved away from the dock.

I'm doing it! He pushed the lever forward a little more, and the engine purred more loudly. He looked around and saw boats scattered throughout the harbor. None was close to him, but he kept careful watch.

With clear water all around him, Jacob pushed the throttle a bit more. A strong breeze whipped at his hair. Small waves slapped at the sides of his boat. Shorebirds darted and dove in the still-humid air.

He had dreamed of this. At last, he was charting his own course. He felt as free as the birds.

Jacob worked the following day but had Sunday off. He decided to go back down to the harbor and take his boat out again.

His parents were both off work, but he didn't want to ask them for a ride because then he might feel obliged to take them out in his boat, and he didn't feel quite ready for that.

So he decided to take a train to the harbor the next morning. He would have to walk about a mile to Jefferson Park, but the train would get him to the harbor in about 30 minutes and cost only five bucks.

He got up early, packed a lunch and took off for Jefferson Park. At the station, he bought a ticket and boarded the 8:57 train.

Liberation gleamed in the bright morning light. Jacob took her out and this time explored more of the harbor, always on watch for other boats, careful to steer clear of them.

He slowly approached the harbor's stone breakwater walls. They ran north and south, with a big gap in between, the entry point to Lake Michigan.

A majestic, white lighthouse stood at the southern end of the northern wall. Jacob had seen it from the roof of the MCC. From there, it looked so small. Now it towered like a church steeple.

He got close to the portal between the harbor walls but stopped. He felt drawn to the Great Lake but, at the same time, not ready for it, as if he were waiting for someone to accompany him.

Around noon, Jacob found a quiet spot with a good view of the lake. He cut his engine and unpacked his lunch. The August sun reddened his neck and arms. Sweating, he took off his shirt, pulled out a can of sunscreen and sprayed his bare skin.

Biting into an apple, Jacob reflected on the improbable arc of his life. It had been a long series of low points. But now, Jacob realized these low points had become pivot points.

Through his loneliness, he had come to know connectedness. Through his despair, he had learned to hope. Through his sense of worthlessness, he had learned to believe in himself.

Maybe his life was meant to be a succession of low points and pivot points like these. Maybe he just needed to learn how to shift gears.

He took the train back to Jefferson Park around three. He needed to be at Sophia's place for dinner at five, and he wanted to buy her flowers, or at least a rose, on the way.

On the train ride, Jacob wondered how long he would need to stay with his parents before he got a place of his own. After only a few weeks of working at Portage Grounds, he had saved more than $1,000. He'd even made the first monthly payment on his boat loan.

Soon, he hoped, he would have enough to rent an apartment. He'd love to get a place near Sophia. He could buy an e-bike to get to work.

He thought about college too. He'd been so close to starting at Wilbur Wright when he had his accident. But why not go for an undergraduate degree from a four-year college? Why not shift gears?

As the train pulled into the station, Jacob slipped his backpack over his shoulder. Despite the sunscreen, his back was badly sunburned. Even though his pack was light, the pressure from the strap caused a stab of pain.

But that pain also reminded Jacob of the joy of floating like a leaf on the water, which not long ago had seemed beyond his reach. Now, as he stepped off the train, he felt grateful and amazed his dreams were coming true.

CHAPTER THIRTY

THE FOLLOWING SUNDAY, Jacob got up early. He was too excited to sleep. This was the day when Sophia and Mateo would finally join him on his boat.

He had taken it out several times over the past week. One evening, he'd taken his parents out. As usual, he'd stayed in the harbor. Today he felt called to go a little farther.

It was a brilliant, cloudless morning. Jacob watched for Sophia and Mateo from the front porch of his parents' house. He was thrilled to see them pull into the driveway in Sophia's SUV.

She lowered her window.

"Good morning!" she said with a big smile.

"Good morning," he said.

"You can throw your stuff in the back."

She released the hatch, and he slid his backpack in beside a cooler. Sophia had insisted on packing their lunch.

Getting in, Jacob turned around and saw Mateo in a booster seat.

"Good morning, young man," he said.

"Good morning."

"Are you ready to go out on a boat?"

"Yeah!"

Jacob fondly remembered his father taking him out on a boat as a boy. It was only a rowboat, but what a thrill. Now Jacob was excited knowing Mateo was in for a thrill like that.

About 45 minutes later, they arrived at the marina. Jacob hopped out, pulled out the cooler and threw his backpack over his shoulder.

"This way," he said.

They walked down a pier to where his boat was docked.

"There she is," Jacob said.

"She's beautiful," Sophia said.

"Lib ...," Mateo said slowly.

"Liberation," Sophia said.

"What does that mean?"

"It means being set free," she said, smiling at Jacob.

"Let me put the cooler onboard and grab Mateo's life jacket," Jacob said. "Then I'll help you in."

He stowed the cooler behind the swivel seats in the cockpit, then went up to the bow and grabbed a small life jacket from under the seat.

"Here you go," he said, handing it to Mateo. "You'll need to put that on before you get on board."

Sophia helped Mateo put it on. Then Jacob reached up for her hand. She slipped her small hand in his and smiled, and he felt his heart racing.

He then helped Mateo on board and took him up to a bench seat in the open bow.

"You can lead the way from up here," Jacob said.

"Cool!"

"I'll untie us," Jacob said, stepping back up onto the dock.

He unwound the stern line from a cleat, then the bow line, and stepped back onboard.

"Excuse me," he said as he squeezed by Sophia.

There wasn't much room, and she put her hands on his waist. For a moment, they were so close that the front of their bare legs touched. They stood still, locked eyes and smiled.

Jacob scooted by but wished he could have lingered. He sat down in his captain's seat and slipped on a pair of sunglasses.

"Before we shove off, let me go over a couple of quick safety procedures," he said.

The main thing was that Sophia knew her life vest was next to her seat in case of an emergency. He also showed her how to work the throttle and two-way radio in the unlikely event he could no longer drive.

"Any questions?"

"Nope!" Mateo said.

"All set," Sophia said.

"Okay. Hang on."

He turned the ignition key, and the engine rumbled to a start.

"Woo!" yelled Mateo.

Jacob lowered a small lever to idle the engine for a moment, then pushed it all the way down. Then he pressed a red button and pulled the throttle back, and the boat began to move away from the dock. When it was clear, he pushed the throttle forward, and they slowly headed into the harbor.

"This is so exciting!" Sophia said.

The harbor was bustling with dinghies, bass boats and small yachts. Jacob kept careful watch and steered clear. The harbor was familiar to him now, and he was tempted to give his guests a tour.

But he knew it was the lake they wanted to see, so he throttled forward as they approached the stone wall at the outer edge of the harbor.

Just ahead stood the lighthouse. In the morning light, the ruby-red lantern at the top sparkled like a gemstone. Mateo got up and pointed excitedly at the great tower.

"Look!" he cried, turning back toward his mother. He was laughing and bobbing up and down. "Look!"

Sophia told him to sit down, but his laughter made her laugh. Jacob looked over at her. The sun lit up her face. He had never seen her look so happy.

He pushed the throttle a little more, and Liberation passed through the breakwater walls. For the first time, she was out of the harbor and on the Great Lake.

Jacob closed his eyes. He hadn't been thinking about Emma. But in that moment, he felt her presence. It was as though she had been there all along, waiting for him.

And he realized Emma had not been in Limbo. It was he who had been in Limbo. He had been confined by a lack of self-confidence, by a fear of the world, by a belief he didn't matter.

Jacob opened his eyes and saw open water all around him. His confinement was over. He pushed the throttle forward firmly and felt a boundless freedom in his soul.

Looking at Sophia, Jacob held out his hand, and she took it.

"I love you," he said.

"And I love you."

OTHER STORIES

MY NAME IS TAYLOR

TAYLOR HEARD low voices outside her bedroom door, then a light knock.

"Come in," she said.

She knew it must be her parents, but she couldn't recall the last time they'd come to her room together.

The door opened, and there they stood, close to one another. They looked uncomfortable.

"I hope we're not interrupting," her mother said.

"You're not," said Taylor.

Her parents slowly stepped in. Taylor was sitting at her desk in the only chair in the room. Her parents looked around, as if searching for somewhere to sit, then sat down next to each other on her bed.

"Taylor, honey, we have some news," her mother said.

One of them has cancer, Taylor thought.

"Is everything okay?"

"Oh, honey," said her mother, in a tone fit for a child, "we're fine."

"Yes," said her father. "We're fine."

"Honey," her mother said, "as you know, Daddy is retiring at the end of the year. And we ..."

Her mother looked away.

"And we've decided it's time to downsize," her father said.

"Downsize?"

"Honey, this is just more house than we need," her mother said, her voice trembling.

"We're looking at condos," her father said, "and we wanted you to know."

Taylor struggled to get her mind around what her parents were saying. As if he sensed this, her father cut to the chase.

"We think this would be a good time for you to find your own place," he said.

Now Taylor got it, and it hit her hard. This was the only place she'd ever lived. Where would she go? What could she afford? Who would care for her?

Taylor felt dizzy, and she must have looked shaken because her parents got up and put their arms around her.

Holding them tight, Taylor thought: how will I live without Mother and Daddy?

———

Over the next couple of weeks, Taylor's parents took turns taking her around to look at apartments. On her salary as a data entry clerk, Taylor couldn't afford much. But living alone, she didn't need much. After all, she worked remotely and spent most of her time in her bedroom, which served as her office.

After looking at half a dozen places, Taylor decided to rent a studio apartment. It was just one room, but it had a large window that looked out over some water. It was only a retaining pond, but ducks swam on it, and at least it offered a glimpse of nature.

It reminded Taylor of the hikes her father had taken her and her older brother and sister on when they were kids. Taylor had loved those hikes. If she closed her eyes, she could still smell the pines, hear the birdsongs, feel the cold creek water against her bare legs and feet.

Best of all, her father had included her. Even as a young girl, Taylor sensed she was slowing the others down, but they always seemed happy she was there.

That was a long time ago and one of the last times Taylor felt like she belonged. Over the course of her 32 years, she'd become more and more alone. She'd never had many friends. She'd never been on a date. In her work, she'd never actually met any of her colleagues, not even her boss.

As her few real relationships fell away, virtual connections took their place. By the time Taylor graduated from high school, she spent much of her time online. The internet had become her closest companion.

When her brother and sister left home, Taylor's parents were still working, and she spent even more time alone. Not that she wanted to be alone. But she found it stressful to be with people. Her social skills, never strong, had atrophied and, with them, her self confidence.

Taylor knew she'd become a recluse and a bit of a mystery. Once, when she was shopping for clothes with her mom, she saw two women who looked vaguely familiar. They were staring at her, and she heard one of them say, "Isn't that ..."

The sad reality, of course, was that Taylor was far from the only young person who was alone. There were simply fewer young people around. Even if Taylor had been a social butterfly, other young butterflies had become rare.

But while her social skills might have been lacking, Taylor's mind was sharp. She was detail-oriented and a computer whiz, and her typing skills were excellent. Her mom once timed her at 80 words per minute.

Knowing this and how shy Taylor was and her lack of interest in college, her father suggested she look into getting a job in data entry. One of his colleagues did this for his company. He talked with her and learned people were doing this type of work for various companies and many of them were doing it remotely. This could be just right for Taylor, he thought. After all, she didn't drive.

But when he mentioned it to her, Taylor initially resisted, mainly because getting a job meant doing an interview, and that idea freaked her out.

"I'll tell you what," her father said. "If you get an interview, I'll coach you through it. We'll practice until you're ready. Besides, anyone hiring a data entry person is mainly interested in how well you can process information and how fast you can type. You'd blow them away."

Taylor hated the idea of being interviewed, but she also knew she needed to get a job, and the prospect of working from home did appeal to her. So she agreed to practice interviewing with her father and *then* apply for a job.

They spent hours practicing, going over answers to every likely question many times. Just in case their was a test during her interview, her father even gave Taylor physical documents like bills and had her type the data into spreadsheets as he watched.

After a few weeks, Taylor began to grow comfortable with these mock interviews, and she surprised herself with how good she was at transferring data from paper documents into a digital database.

I can do this, she thought, although she wouldn't allow herself to say so out loud.

In the meantime, her father had found several open positions for data entry clerks, all of them for companies in the area. Taylor had to admit she was ready to apply, and her father helped her do so online.

Within days, she got two invitations to come in to interview — and take a test.

"Now what am I going to do?" she said anxiously.

"You're going to knock their socks off," her father said, giving her a hug.

He drove Taylor to both interviews. Both companies offered her jobs on the spot. Fortunately, she'd talked about that possibility with her father, and they'd agreed she would think about it and follow up.

That evening, Taylor told her parents all about her experience that day. In recounting it aloud, she realized one of the interviewers had paid much closer attention to what she had to say. She seemed more respectful. Ultimately, that made the difference for Taylor. The following morning, she called "the winner" to accept.

Now, 14 years later, she was still doing the same data entry job for the same company, which handled work for more than a dozen clients.

In all that time, Taylor had never had to leave her bedroom to do the work. Her employer sent her envelopes and boxes of forms by courier every few days, Taylor entered mountains of data into her computer and her employer received everything in digital form. Once a month, someone came to collect all the old materials.

Taylor was meticulous in her work. Not once did she ever receive a complaint or hear a concern. Her employer gave her good reviews, which were always conducted by email, and a three percent raise every year. Every two years, she got a new computer.

But no one from the company ever called Taylor or asked her to come into the office. This only deepened her sense of isolation, and it made her wonder if, beyond reliably and efficiently entering data, she meant anything to anyone in the real world.

Now Taylor spent most of her time in her small apartment. She didn't own a car and still hadn't learned to drive. She had her groceries delivered. Five times a week, she walked or jogged on a treadmill, a gift from her parents. At night, she usually watched movies or documentaries on Netflix.

During the warmer weather months, she had begun going outside to sit on a bench overlooking the retaining pond. She liked to watch the ducks. She fed them old bread.

Over time, she got to know the ducks. Most were mallards, but she learned to tell them apart. By watching them, she discovered each had its own way of swimming and quacking. Each had its own pace and temperament. Most would waddle up close to her. A few hung back, despite the prospect of easy food.

Sometimes, if no one was around, Taylor would call the ducks by name. She named them all. Everyone and everything deserves a name, she thought. Except for her parents and occasionally her siblings, no one called Taylor by name anymore.

Sometimes her company would address her by name in emails. And of course bills and ads arrived in her mailbox bearing her name. But there's a big difference between seeing your name and hearing it spoken. There is something inside each of us that longs to hear someone saying our name.

———

One night, as she was getting ready for bed, Taylor looked at herself in a small mirror on the wall. In the bright light of the lamp on her bedstand, she saw small wrinkles in the skin at the corners of her eyes. Leaning in, she spotted a few strands of gray in her hair and noticed creases under her cheeks.

I'm getting old, she thought. Will I always be alone? Will I die here? When I'm gone, will anyone even care?

She sat down on her bed and began to cry. Feeling lonely down to her bones, Taylor wept until she fell asleep.

———

One warm and sunny Saturday morning, Taylor was feeding the ducks when she saw something out the corner of her eye. Something or someone had gone by just beyond some trees that bordered the property of her apartment complex. She decided to check it out.

As Taylor approached the trees, she could see bicycles passing by, and she realized she'd seen someone riding a bike. As she reached the edge of the stand of trees, she saw an asphalt path on the other side.

She stepped onto a swath of grass between the trees and the path and watched bike riders whiz past. She looked down the path and saw two women walking toward her. She stepped onto the path and slowly walked toward them. When they had nearly reached her, they both said, "Good morning." It might only have been bike trail etiquette, but it sure did make Taylor feel good.

"Good morning," she replied.

Taylor kept walking. She crossed paths with a dozen walkers and runners, all of whom said hello. Even most of the bikers who sped past acknowledged her, if only with a nod. How refreshing, Taylor thought.

About a mile down the trail, Taylor came to a bench. It was getting hot, and she was tired and thirsty. She decided to sit down on the bench in the shade of a big elm tree.

Taylor spotted a runner in the distance, coming toward her. At first, she couldn't tell if it was a man or a woman. But soon she realized it was a man.

As he got closer, she could see he was a young man, maybe about her age. He was wearing red shorts and a white T-shirt. He was drenched in sweat, and his shirt clung to his lean upper body like plastic wrap.

"Good morning," he said with a smile.

"Good morning."

Passing by, he said, "Have a great day."

"You too," Taylor called after him.

She watched him as he ran down the trail with an easy stride, neither fast nor slow. For a moment, she imagined running alongside him.

She watched him until he was out of sight, and although she sat alone, for the first time in a long time, Taylor did not feel lonely.

———

The following Saturday morning, Taylor sat in the shade on that same bench, hoping the young man might run by again.

Lots of bikers and walkers and a handful of runners passed by, but there was no sign of the young man. Taylor knew it was long shot.

After waiting an hour, this time sipping water from a bottle she'd brought along, she got up and started walking back down the trail. A few minutes later, she heard footsteps behind her. She turned around. It was him.

In that moment, she reflexively looked at his left hand, in which he held a bottle of Gatorade. No ring.

"Good morning again," he said with a big smile.

He remembers me, Taylor thought.

"Good morning," she said as he ran by.

He was at least a head taller than Taylor.

"Have a good one," he said, with a little wave.

"You too!"

He was again drenched in sweat, and the smell of it, mixed with the fragrance of soap, hung in the air. For some reason, it reminded Taylor of hiking in the woods as a girl, and she felt warm inside.

Once again, she watched him until he was out of sight, and she again imagined running alongside him. That thought too gave her a warm feeling inside.

The following Saturday morning, Taylor went back to the bench, hoping, praying he might run by again. It was already getting hot, so she got there about an hour early, just in case he decided to beat the heat.

She sat sipping cold water, grateful for the shade, watching people pass by, but there was no sign of him. She kept looking at her watch. The previous two Saturdays, he'd run through there by now.

"You're crazy," she whispered to no one.

Then she let out a small laugh. Not a happy laugh. But a laugh at the absurdity of her situation. Was she so desperate to meet someone, so lonely, that it had come to this? And even if this guy shows up, what are the chances of ever even meeting him?

Tears formed in her eyes and fell down her cheeks. She wiped them away with the back of her hand in case anyone passing by might see. But Taylor was sad. She was sad to be so disconnected from the real world. She was sad that, even out amongst people, she knew none of them and none of them knew her. She was sad that she might spend the rest of her life alone, processing data for faceless people she would never meet.

Just then, she saw someone running toward her. It was him! She wiped her cheeks again, sat up straighter and scooted down the bench a little to leave room, just in case.

When he was about 20 feet away, he stopped running. He started walking and wiped the sweat from his face. This time, he carried no Gatorade.

"Hello again," he said with big, bright smile.

"Hello again," Taylor said, smiling too.

When he got to the bench, he stopped.

"Would you mind if I sat for a minute?"

"Not at all," Taylor said, inching over just a little.

He sat down next to her. His hair was black and rather long. His face was covered with stubble, and he too had small wrinkles at the corners of his eyes, which were light green with a hint of blue, the color of a cool creek on a hot summer day.

In a crowd, he might blend in. But at that moment, no one else was around, and Taylor thought he was the most handsome man she had ever seen.

Turning toward her, he said, "I'm Jason."

He started to extend his hand, which was sweaty but, looking embarrassed, he wiped his palm across his shorts.

"It's okay," she said with a small laugh.

Then she took his hand and said, "My name is Taylor."

EVERYONE WINS

NICK STOOD in the opening of the HR director's cubicle and waited for her to turn around and greet him. When she kept working at her desk, he cleared his throat to get her attention.

She swiveled around in her chair and looked up at him, then looked at her watch.

"You were supposed to be here 15 minutes ago," she said.

"Sorry," Nick said.

"Sorry?"

"I got hung up."

Nicole, the HR director, shook her head, picked up a folder and stood up.

"Let's go to a meeting room across the hall," she said.

Uh oh, Nick thought. This can't be good.

He followed her into a meeting room, and she closed the door behind him.

"Have a seat," she said.

Nick pulled out a chair and sat down. Nicole went around

the table and sat down across from him. She started to open the folder in front of her, then closed it and placed one hand over the other on top of it. She leaned in slightly and looked Nick in the eye.

"Nick, this just isn't working out," she said.

"What?" he said, tilting his head and smiling a little.

"Your job, Nick."

"My job?"

"Yes. We're letting you go."

Nick was stunned.

"What?"

"Nick, I don't think this should come as a surprise. You've been on a performance improvement plan for three months," she said, patting the folder. "But we've seen no improvement. If anything, your performance has gotten worse. I'm afraid you've left us no choice."

Nick had feared something like this might happen. And yet, he had told himself it would not happen because nothing like it had ever happened to him. He'd led a charmed life in which every door had been opened to him and he could do no wrong.

"You're a winner," he'd been told from time he started playing T-ball. At age four, he could barely hold the bat, let alone swing it. And yet, at the end of the season, like all the other players, he got a trophy. Nick brought his home and put it in his bedroom, where, over the years, he would display dozens of trophies. Most of the plates were either engraved with "Participation" or left blank.

Nick had sailed through college, which his parents had paid for, and lined up this job even before he graduated. He'd never had a job before or been responsible for much at all. Even now, he was driving his parents' spare car to work and still living at home.

Everybody was thrilled when he landed this job, and at first the company seemed happy to have him. But then his boss, Stephanie, began getting testy with Nick about the smallest things, like missing deadlines and showing up late for meetings.

On his first day, Stephanie had told Nick about his job and what would be expected of him. But he thought it was only a bunch of corporate speak. After all, he might be late, but he was there, and in Nick's life, that had always been enough.

Now Nicole opened the folder in front of her, reached in and pulled out a check, which she slid across the table.

"This is your final paycheck, Nick, plus two weeks of severance pay," she said. "Good luck."

———

Driving home, Nick felt nauseous. What was he going to tell his parents? When he got this job, they'd told everybody their son had made good. How would his getting fired after only six months reflect on them?

Nick was still trying to make sense of it. He had always believed everybody should be treated equally, regardless of their performance. He had simply assumed he would be successful in the "real world." But now he was out. What did this say about him?

"You're a loser," Nick said under his breath, afraid that saying it any louder might be too much to bear.

———

When Nick got home, his parents were still at work. He decided to go up to his room and take a nap.

He was awakened by a knock at his door. He opened his eyes

and had to think about where he was and why he was there. Then he remembered what had happened at work. He wanted to go back to sleep but heard his door creaking open.

"Nick," his mother said, peeking around the edge of the door, "are you okay?"

"Yeah, Mom. I'm okay."

Still holding the door knob, she said, "Have you been home for a while?"

"Yeah," Nick said, sitting up and swinging his legs over the side of the bed.

"Did you get off work early?"

"Yeah."

"Is everything okay?"

"Actually, no, Mom, it's not."

"What's wrong?" she said, stepping into the room.

Looking down at the floor, Nick said, "I got fired."

"What?" she said with a small laugh.

"I got fired," he said. "Seriously."

"Oh, Nick. I'm sorry. What happened?"

As he told his mother about his meeting with Nicole that morning, Nick felt like an utter failure. He had never felt this way before.

"Don't worry," his mother said, wrapping her arms around him and kissing him on the head. "You'll get another job. You'll show them."

When his mother had left to make dinner, Nick looked over at all his trophies. His father had built shelves for them, and one wall was nearly covered with trophies.

Growing up, Nick had loved looking at them. Now they were a reminder that he hadn't really achieved anything.

He got up and stepped over to the window. He opened the blinds and looked out over his backyard.

There were the swing set and the fire pit and the garden, just as they were when he was a boy. Nothing had ever really changed here. Nor had he. Nick had always felt so good about himself. Wherever he went, people liked him. It was if he could do no wrong.

Until now. Now he felt worthless, and he had no idea what to do.

Then he heard the garage door go up. His father was home. He had always been so proud of Nick, his only child, the little boy who could do no wrong. But what would he think of his little boy now?

He heard voices downstairs, the unmistakable creak of the stairs under his father's feet and a knock at his door.

"Come in."

Nick got up and turned his chair around.

His father came in and closed the door behind him.

"Nick," he said, "I'm sorry."

"Thanks, Dad."

His father stepped over to the bed and sat down.

"What happened?" he said.

Nick looked down at the floor.

"If you'd rather not talk about it ..."

"No, it's okay."

Nick told him what had happened at work that morning. His father listened carefully and, for the first time, asked Nick about his job.

Nick told him all about it, including how he had struggled from the start. Sharing these things with his father, who had been so successful in his career, Nick felt ashamed. He felt he had let his father down.

But his father said, "It's my fault."

"What?"

"Nick, when I was growing up, I had a lot of, well, challenges, and I wanted your life to be different. I wanted it to be easy. But now I realize I made it too easy. That's why you weren't ready for that job, and that's on me."

His father looked so sad, as if he could cry.

"You're being too hard on yourself," Nick said.

"I should have been tougher."

"You're a good father."

His father was staring at the floor.

"Dad, what do you think I should do?"

His father blinked and looked up.

"Do what you like. Get good at it, and people will know they can depend on you."

"But I'm not good at anything."

"You haven't really tried."

"But I have, Dad. I tried, and I failed. I'm a failure."

"You're not a failure, Nick. Just because this job didn't work out doesn't mean you can't succeed. You've just got to find the right job for you. And whatever job that is, no matter how good you are at it, just know you're going to have setbacks. You're going to make mistakes. But that's how we learn and grow."

———

The following morning, once his parents had left for work, Nick decided to take a walk. It was a sunny but chilly fall day. He slipped on a jacket and cap, locked the front door behind him and headed out.

He walked down his street. It was fun to see the houses of his old friends. He wondered if any of them still lived there.

He walked past his old school and the grocery store where

he used to buy candy and sometimes pick up a few things for his mom. Then he came upon a field where he used to play soccer. A sign on the fence read: Everyone Wins.

Nick had played soccer there his whole childhood. No one ever kept score, and everyone "won" every game. And all the players got "participation trophies" at the end of the season.

Nick wasn't very good at soccer. He never scored a goal. Now he wished he had learned to play better. The teams in that league had coaches, but they never really did much. After all, what's the point of coaching when everyone wins?

As he started walking back home, Nick thought about what he should do now. "Do what you like," his father had said. Nick had always liked numbers. That's why he'd majored in finance in college.

When he got home, Nick went upstairs and got online. He found dozens of finance and accounting positions posted on various job sites. Several were local. Nearly all were remote.

All applications were online, and Nick began applying. When it came to his employment history, he felt uneasy but figured anyone interested would find out he was let go.

He filled out and submitted about 10 applications that day, and he kept going the following morning. He did the same the following three mornings until he had submitted applications to about 50 companies. With so many lines in the water, he thought, he was sure to get some bites.

But he was wrong. A week later, he'd gotten only a handful of responses, all of them rejections. He suspected companies had checked with his former employer and learned the truth. He could never know for sure, but he gave up trying to find a job in finance or accounting.

One morning, bummed and not sure what to do next, Nick

went into town to a grab coffee at the Cozy Brew Cafe. "We're hiring," said a sign in the window.

Nick had never thought about working in a coffee shop, but he loved coffee. As he waited for his latte, he asked the young lady who took his order how he might apply. She handed him an application.

"Just fill it out," she said with a smile.

When his latte was ready, Nick grabbed it, sat down at a table and looked over the application. There was an employment history section, marked "If Applicable." Nick decided to leave it blank.

When he'd finished his coffee, he went back to the counter and handed the young lady his application.

"Thanks," she said. "Our manager will be in this afternoon. I'll make sure she gets this."

"Thank you," Nick said.

The following morning, he got a called from the manager, whose name was Ana. She asked him to come in for an interview.

Nick went in that afternoon. He met Ana, whom he guessed to be about 40. They went over to a table to talk. Ana mainly wanted to tell Nick about the cafe and answer any questions he had.

She did ask about his employment history, and Nick told her the truth. He thought that might be the end of the interview.

But instead, Ana said, "So what did you learn from that experience?"

"A lot," Nick said. "But the main thing is to make sure I'm in the right job."

Ana smiled.

"Do you think working here as a barista might be the right job for you?" she said.

"I'd love the opportunity to find out."

"Good. When can you start?"

Nick reported for work the following morning. Ana was there to greet him. She introduced him to his new co-workers, including a young woman named Emily. She was the head barista and would be his trainer.

At first, Nick was a bit overwhelmed by all the coffee machines and the different orders. But Emily was a patient teacher. For two weeks, she stayed close to Nick, coaching, correcting and encouraging him until he got the hang of it.

Soon Nick was making coffee drinks on his own. He was careful and precise but slow. Orders began to pile up, and customers were getting upset.

"You're going to have to step it up," Emily told him.

A few weeks earlier, Nick would have nodded and done nothing differently. He might have even taken umbrage and sworn at his boss under his breath.

But now, maybe for the first time in his life, Nick felt responsible for something. This was his job, and people were depending on him. He didn't want to hold anyone up, so he worked hard to go faster and keep up with orders.

By going faster, Nick made mistakes. But Emily was there to help him learn from those mistakes so he could improve. Listening to Emily, Nick also heard his father's voice.

Six months later, Ana left to take another job, and Emily took on her role as manager of the cafe. The first thing she did was promote Nick as her successor. He was ecstatic.

"You're ready," she said with a smile, "and you've earned it."

That night, lying in bed in his apartment, Nick thought about his experience at Cozy Brew and marveled at how much he'd changed.

All his life, he'd believed everyone wins. But what he was

learning is that, when everyone wins, nobody improves or learns to be accountable for anything, and everyone takes a hit.

If everyone wins, no one wins, Nick thought, as he drifted off to sleep.

THE MOMENT

I'LL NEVER FORGET the moment it happened. I was scarfing down a bowl of Frosted Flakes, scrolling through TikTok, when "lost connection" flashed on my screen.

As I went to the bottom of the stairs to call up to Mom, I was swearing under my breath.

"The router's down again!"

"I'll fix it, Noah," Mom said, emerging from her bedroom and stepping down the hallway.

I felt anxious. I needed to leave for school in a few minutes, and sometimes our system took longer than that to come back online.

I'd been about to watch Zach King's Magic Ride, a video about a guy named Zach King performing magic tricks. Everybody at school was talking about it. I'd meant to check it out earlier but forgot. Now I'd be the only one who hadn't seen it. Not cool when you're 16.

I went back into the kitchen, finished my cereal and downed

my orange juice. As I headed upstairs to grab my stuff, Mom was coming down.

"I rebooted it," she said.

What a relief.

In the car, I pressed TikTok on my phone, but there was still no connection. I'll try it again when I get to school, I thought.

But when I got there, everybody was standing around, shaking their heads and tapping their phones. Mornings at school were usually quiet. Everyone was still waking up. That morning, though, an awful din pervaded the place.

A buzzer sounded, and we all shuffled to our homerooms. As we sat down, many kids were still tapping their phones and grumbling. Then we heard the click of the PA system, and everyone got quiet.

"Good morning."

It was our principal, Mr. Hill. He was a real hard-ass. He always spoke with authority, but that morning, he sounded shaken.

"By now you all know we're experiencing issues with our Wi-Fi connection. So if you have a smartphone, it won't work. Our IT guy is on it, and we hope to have the system back up soon. In the meantime, anyone who normally uses a laptop for class will have to use a textbook. Fortunately, our landline phones here in the office still work. So if you need to make a call, come to the office. I'm sure we'll be back online soon. In the meantime, let's all be patient."

Click. Everyone looked around at each other. Many of my classmates started tapping their phones again, as if that would snap them back to life. Nervous chatter filled the room.

"Okay," Mrs. Frederickson, our homeroom teacher, said. "Quiet."

Mrs. Frederickson was a hard-ass too, and the room got quiet.

I moved through that day feeling like I was in a kind of netherworld. Reading from textbooks and writing with a pen felt foreign. I was so used to checking my phone that I kept pulling it out of my pocket, even though I knew it was of no use.

We all left school that day on edge. On the way home, I turned on my car radio and listened to the news. Apparently, the internet was down everywhere, and nobody knew why. It felt like a bad dream.

When I got home, my parents were still at work. I went up to my room and turned on my laptop. Still no connection.

When my parents got home, I found out their days had been no better than mine. They both relied on their computers at work, so they got very little done.

We had dinner in the family room, watching CNN. Reporting about the internet crash, which had happened all around the world, was non-stop. Teams of experts were working frantically to pinpoint the source of the problem.

Our phone rang. Not a cell phone, but our old house phone in the kitchen. We hadn't used it in years. I was amazed it still worked.

Mom got up to get it. She came back a few minutes later.

"Who was that?" Dad said.

"Emily Williams. She was calling to let me know school is cancelled for tomorrow. Fewer people on the roads, I guess. Then I had to call the Fisks to let them know."

Dad smiled.

"The old phone chain," he said.

"Yeah. I've haven't had to call anybody like that since Michael and Sarah were in grade school."

I had no idea what they were talking about, except that I was off school the next day.

Over the course of the evening, news coverage of the outage got more concerning. There were stories about the halt in online banking and stock trading, flight delays and cancellations and power outages. The coverage also got darker, including speculation about cyberterrorism.

Finally, after a story about our national defense systems being at risk, Dad turned off the TV. He looked worried.

"Why don't we all get some sleep?" he said.

We got up, and Mom came over and gave me a hug. It had been a long time since anyone had hugged me.

We all went upstairs.

"I'm sure we'll be back online in the morning," Dad said.

As I lay in bed, I thought about that chaotic day. I thought about the concern in Mr. Hill's voice, in my classmates' faces, in my parents' eyes. But I also thought about the surprising satisfaction I got from seeing my own handwriting in my classes at school.

———

In the morning, I awoke with the sun and instinctively reached for my phone. Still no signal. I felt so alone, so cut off from the world.

I went downstairs. Dad was watching news in the family room. The hearty aroma of pancakes and coffee wafted in from the kitchen.

"Any good news?" I asked.

"No. The internet's still down."

"Do they know why?"

"No, but there's now speculation that AI is to blame."

"AI?"

"Yeah. Sounds like something out of sci-fi movie, doesn't it?"

Dad laughed a small laugh, but I detected a nervousness in his voice. He was usually so calm. I sensed this disruption had really spooked him. I wondered if he was afraid of losing his job. I wondered if he was afraid for me.

"You guys hungry?" Mom called from the kitchen.

"Well, we might as well eat," Dad said. "Looks like we won't be doing much today."

He got up and managed a faint smile. I wondered if he was putting on a brave face for me.

The three of us sat down around the kitchen table. We hadn't shared a meal in a long time.

"Why don't you start, Noah?" Mom said, passing me a plate of fluffy pancakes.

"Thank you," I said, taking it.

I plopped three pancakes onto my plate.

"So," I said, pouring syrup on my pancakes, "tell me what life was like before the internet."

Mom smiled.

"We played board games," she said.

"And read newspapers," said Dad.

For an hour they regaled me with stories of what life was like in the "old days." As they did, their tension seemed to ease and, to me, the prospect of being unplugged seemed rather inviting.

———

The internet didn't come back that day. Or the next day. Or the next.

Experts worked 24/7 to find a fix. They couldn't come up with one, but they did determine AI caused the shutdown. They tried to disable it or find a work-around, but they were unsuccessful. AI was always one step ahead.

With no solution in sight, we all began to resign ourselves to the idea that we'd have to figure out how to live, at least temporarily, offline.

The adjustment was monumental. Without cell phones, we had to use landline telephones. Without email, we had to mail letters. Without Amazon, we had to buy stuff in stores. Without Google, we had to go to libraries. Without online news, we had to read newspapers, watch TV or listen to the radio. Without ATMs, we had to go to the bank to get money.

I'd never had to write much by hand. When I did, I printed. But taking notes in class, I quickly learned that printing was too slow, so I had to write in cursive. It took me a while to get the hang of that.

Same for reading books. When I started reading *The Pearl* by John Steinbeck, I tried to swipe the page instead of turning it. It was the first book I'd held in my hands since I was a boy. I'd nearly forgotten the sweet, earthy smell of a book.

But the biggest change for me was learning how to live without social media. It had been with me all my life. Over the years, it had *become* my way of life.

When Covid hit, five years ago, and I had to stay home and "go to school" online, I felt so isolated. I was in the fifth grade. My brother and sister, who were in high school, seemed to be able to adjust. But being alone rocked my world. My real-life friendships went dormant. Now if I wanted to connect with anybody, I had to go online.

Over the next few years, a lot of people grew content, even happy, to live in this virtual world. But not me. I felt lonely and sad. I suspect I was depressed, but I didn't talk with anyone about it because I wasn't sure who I could trust.

But when the internet went down, now more than a year ago, people began talking to one another again, and I gladly joined in those conversations. I renewed old friendships and made new friends. I started hanging out with other kids, going over to their houses, going to movies. I joined the track team. I went on dates.

Of course, losing the internet caused real problems too, especially for the economy. But after a few months of being offline, everyone began to adjust, and life went on.

———

Yesterday, for a reason that at this point is unclear, the internet came back up.

"It's like AI just decided to let go," one expert said. "Like it had toyed with us long enough."

I suspect we'll all get back online again, and soon everything will be a lot like it was. No more need to write letters or shop in stores or even leave our homes. Life will no doubt be more efficient.

But I've decided I'm going to stay unplugged a little longer. Yesterday, I finished third in the mile at a big track meet and made it home in time to have dinner with my parents. Afterwards, I fell asleep reading a book, a paperback.

ACKNOWLEDGMENTS

I am deeply grateful to my wife Liz, Kathy Kennedy, Patti Normile, Libby Belle, Christine des Garennes, Dee Lorraine, John Young, Ed Kruszynski and Gordon Lawrie for their helpful feedback on drafts of this novella.

I also want to thank Maggie Toerner for her wonderful cover design and Beth Anderson and Jon Virgi for their expert formatting.

Don Tassone is the author of two novels, a novella, a children's book and nine short story collections. He and his wife Liz live in Loveland, Ohio. They have four children and 12 grandchildren.